NIGHT KNUCKLES

Other Books by B.L. Morgan

Blood and Rain
Blood for the Masses
Blood on Celluloid

NIGHT KNUCKLES

A TWO FISTED ZOMBIE WESTERN

B. L. MORGAN

SPEAKING VOLUMES, LLC

NAPLES, FLORIDA

2011

NIGHT KNUCKLES

ISBN: 978-1-61232-016-8

Library of Congress Control Number: 2010942888

Dedicated to the heroes of my life;
Bob L .Morgan Sr. and Flora Izailia Morgan.

Acknowledgments

I would like to thank the following people for information, inspiration and encouragement;

My wife Judi for unending belief in what I do and a good kick in the ass when I doubt myself.

Paul & Saralyn Fulbright of Ranch/Horse Outfitters.

Lee Pletzers-Excellent author on the rise of mind bending science fiction and horror novels-for much needed encouragement.

Yvonne Navarro-Bestselling award winning author for valued correspondence.

Joe R. Lansdale-Bestselling award winning author-for ideas on how to blend horror and westerns.

The entire gang at Embark To Madness for much needed encouragement and information.

The Tacoma Writer's Meetup Group for much valuable feedback.

All the writers and staff at NANOWRIMO (the novel in a month website) for having their yearly contest every November for providing a lot of incentive to produce a large amount of work fast.

Special thanks: Goes out to Kay Ayres for spotting some errors and giving me reasons as to why some parts work that I had doubts about.

Special thanks: Goes out to the excellent author Holly Catanzarita for a splendid job of editing this novel.

2nd Special thanks goes to Rob Starr for his excellent editing job.

London Prize Ring Rules
Established by Jack Broughton -1743

Contest starts with combatants coming to scratch at the center of the ring.

A round ends when a man is knocked down whereupon he is given thirty seconds to rest and eight additional seconds to come to scratch or be declared the loser.

There is no limit to the number of rounds to be fought.

All fights continue until one man cannot continue and he is declared the loser.

Table of Contents

PROLOGUE:
The Rest Haven Nursing Home
Seattle Washington
Present Day

I'm the guy who comes in at ten PM, five nights a week, empties the trash, sweeps and mops the floors and cleans up any messes that day shift leave for me.

I am the janitor.

I walk the darkened halls of this place where forgotten people come to die.

I mop and sweat and listen to the gasping last breaths of the people who spend their final days here.

On this night I was cleaning up near the last room in the hallway on the east side of the building. All was quiet except for the beeping of a heart monitor in the room I was next to.

Then I heard a weak cough and a quiet gasping call, "Hey, come here for a second will ya?"

I stopped for a moment. It wasn't the first time I'd heard someone in here call out in their sleep. Usually, the smart thing to do is ignore it.

I was going to ignore it. I turned to step away from the door.

"Come on. I'm gonna die soon. Can't an old man at least talk to someone before he goes," the raspy voice called to me. "Is that too much to ask?"

I entered the room where the heart monitor beeped.

The old man was lying in bed. He had all kinds of tubes attached to him and a chemical smell emanated from where he lay. I'm not a doctor or even an orderly so I don't know what the tubes were for.

He lifted a liver spotted hand and beckoned me closer. There was a chair beside the old man's bed. I sat down.

The old man looked at me with red rimmed eyes. I could tell he had not been lying. This man would not be alive very long.

"How are you doing dude?" I asked him.

He gave a short laugh that was more choke than laugh. When he regained his breath he smiled and said, "Just wonderful. Can't you see I'm ready to go run The Boston Marathon?"

"Kind of figured that," I told him.

Then silence filled the air for a full two minutes. When he spoke again his words were full of sadness and regret.

"I called you in here to talk. I haven't talked to anyone for days. They treat us like old busted down machines that they have to keep running. They come in and oil the parts then leave." He wheezed. "Now that I've got you in here, I got nothing to say. Shit, I'll die silent and alone."

"You don't have to talk," I told him. "Save your breath."

That made him laugh. It was a sputtering gasping laugh. "For what?" He coughed. "I've lived a nothing life. At my age I should have something to tell you about what I did, about what I've seen. But I didn't do shit and the things I've seen aren't worth mentioning."

"That's OK," I said and went to stand.

The old man reached out and grabbed my arm and said, "Stay please."

I sat back down.

"If I don't have a story to tell you about my life," he said. "Then I'll tell you a story that my Great Grandpa told me when I was a kid and he said that his Grandpa told it to him. I don't know if it's true, but when I was a kid it sure seemed real to me."

And so the old man talked and I listened.

CHAPTER ONE
Totem Lake Washington
1891

It was a different time back then, a time when there weren't very many automobiles, radio hadn't been invented yet and television ... well no one back then would have dreamed that one day millions of people would stare into boxes where little people danced around.

Washington was a brand new state and there weren't nearly as many people as there are now.

Yes it was a different time but if you wanted a history lesson you'd go take a class at the community college. I'll go ahead and get on with my story.

*　　*　　*

It was after dark and a full grinning moon shined down upon the streets of Totem Lake Washington. Usually at this time of night all the good folk of that little town were at home and in bed and cuddling up, except for the guys getting juiced at Charley's Saloon that is. But we ain't talking about them. We're talking about everybody else, the good hard working people, the people who need to get a good night's rest.

Tonight, nobody was sleeping.

Everybody was at the crossroads of Main Street and Cedar Avenue. Everybody had come out to see a fight.

The crossroads was a big open space in the center of town. It was the center of the business district and all kinds of shops, like the General Store and the Gunsmith's Shop, lined the streets that met at the crossroads.

Except for the drinking establishments all the shops were closed.

In the center of the crossroads four posts had been driven into the ground marking off a large square. Three ropes had been tied and pulled tight between the posts to cordon off the battleground.

Elevated torches on poles illuminated the faces of the crowd that milled around the outside of the ring and the one man who stood at ring center with his hands on his hips.

Black Jack Lonagan barked at the official that stood off to the side leaning on the ropes, "Declare me the winner dam you! I'm here at the mark and the bastard ain't showed his yellow hide."

The referee looked at his watch. "It was agreed the match would start at midnight. He's got three minutes yet. And besides, if I declare there's to be no fight, we're sure to have us a riot."

"Ask me if I give a shit," Lonagan shouted.

There was a sudden hush like a wet blanket had been tossed over the crowd.

The front door to the only large combination hotel and whorehouse in Totem Lake, a place named Hillarie's House of Pleasure flew open. Into the flickering torchlight of the crossroads stepped a small man in a shiny black top hat and a black suit. If you didn't know better you would have thought he was the town undertaker.

Walking behind him was the mighty and mysterious man known only as Night Knuckles.

Night Knuckles was so tall when he walked through the crowd it looked like everyone else was sitting down. His face was stone hard. He had the look of a Greek God that had been sentenced to hell and just recently escaped. His eyes seemed to glow a strange ethereal blue under the hood of his black robe in the flickering torch light.

The referee walked over to Black Jack Lonagan in the center of the ring.

"In about a minute you can tell him yourself that he's a lilly-livered-yellow-bastard," He said.

"Shut your trap," Lonagan told the referee and his voice was none too steady because of trembling lips.

The milling crowd seemed oblivious to the arrival of the second combatant. They stomped around in the crossroads doing their own thing and it looked like it was going to be a fight just to get Night Knuckles and his handler to the ring.

The referee cupped his hands to his mouth and shouted, "Y'all need to get the hell out of the way and let Dr. Abner and Night Knuckles on through if we're gonna be able to have a fight here tonight!"

They paid about as much attention to him as a storm cloud pays attention to the sun that wants to break on through. Those folks were going to move when they were good and ready.

Dr. Abner looked at the roiling sea of humanity between him and the roped off square at the center of the crossroads. He smiled and his white teeth glistened in the moonlight. Dr. Abner extended his right hand in front of him. His fist was closed. His palm was straight up pointing at the moon.

He opened his fist and extended his fingers.

An icy breeze seemed to pass by him and into the crowd and like Moses parted the Red Sea, the people moved aside creating a passage that he and Night Knuckles walked through to the ring.

When they got to the ring Night Knuckles stepped over the top rope and entered the squared circle.

Black Jack Lonagan went back to his corner where his handler helped him out of his robe. He threw a few practice punches into the air to loosen up.

Lonagan was a big man at the height of his physical peak. His muscles rippled as he warmed up. He glanced over his shoulder just as Night Knuckles slipped out of his robe and thought, *Jesus Christ! Is there any way I can get the hell out of this?*

Night Knuckles was a towering colossus. Most big men were somewhat flabby, but not him. He looked like he was made of steel. He was a man-mountain of muscles piled on top of muscles. His arms had the look of bone crushing powerful locomotive pistons.

If that wasn't enough, the look on Night Knuckles face was one of pure cold fury. That look told Lonagan that tonight he meant to kill and it didn't matter who was in front of him. He would do what he came to do.

The referee called them both to the mark at ring center.

Dr. Abner slapped Night Knuckles on the back and told him, "You know what to do. Get out there and do it!"

5

Night Knuckles silently turned and walked.

Lonagan's corner man looked at Night Knuckles. He shook his head and said, "I just want let you know I'll take good care of your horse for you when all this is over. I know you're kind of attached to her and …"

"Shut up!" Lonagan shouted and with trembling knees went to the mark at ring center.

*   *   *

The Indian medicine woman Shingi Notowatakanay Whowhatokanangi came violently awake sitting up. She was used to having visions in her sleep but this one caused her to break out in a cold sweat.

In her dream the medicine woman had seen an enormous ancient spider enter a white man's town. There the spider, that she somehow knew was a male, had given birth to hundreds of other spiders. Those spiders went off and entered the dwellings of the white people and devoured them.

Shingi sat and stared into the dying embers of her fire thinking about what she had seen. She didn't much care for the white men's towns or their ways but what she had seen was pure evil and she could not let it devour an entire town's people without doing something to stop it from happening.

The medicine woman did not know who or what the enormous ancient spider represented. She did not exactly know where the town was; only that it was in her future.

Shingi was an exile from her own people. She tried to warn them of a coming plague. They had not listened and when the people started dying, they blamed Shingi for the disease and cast her out.

The medicine woman knew she would face the evil thing that was somewhere ahead of her. It was the way of her kind. For those who could see, could never turn away.

She stirred the embers into red life and added more wood to the fire until it burned bright and warm. Shingi sat in front of her campfire and waited for dawn. She knew there would be no more sleep tonight.

*   *   *

The referee spoke, "Y'all know the rules; no kicking, no biting, no eye gouging and no hitting the god-dammed referee. I'll tell you right now I don't give a squat about those first three rules but if you hit the god-dammed referee, him being me, I will declare the other man the winner. You got that?"

Both men nodded.

The referee took a step back.

Both men brought their bare fists up in front of their faces.

"Now when I say go," the referee barked, "This fight is on."

Both men locked eyes, although Lonagan was very reluctant to do that and both men nodded again.

"Go!" The referee shouted.

Lonagan leaped forward and slammed a hard overhand right to Night Knuckles' chin. He felt the blow land with sickening force all the way through the muscles of his leg right down to the toes of his right foot as he pushed off from the ground.

It was the kind of punch that broke jaws and necks and sent men's minds into oblivion. Lonagan had used this tactic several times before. When it worked, each time that blow sent the receiver down into the dirt choking on his own blood. But this time it was like punching a stone.

Lonagan jerked his hand back after the hard thwack. It was completely numb except for the lancing pain in the center knuckle.

He wondered if that hand was broken.

And Night Knuckles, his head hadn't even been moved at all.

Lonagan jumped back out of range as Night Knuckles swung a stiff armed left hook that swooshed past his face missing by about an inch. The punch wasn't fast but from the wind that swirled past him he knew he would have been laid out cold if the punch landed.

Lonagan moved away in a semicircle, then without warning leaped forward and threw a hard, fast left-right, left-right to Night Knuckles sides. The punches landed with dull thuds like someone beating on a side of beef with a mallet.

Night Knuckles did not make a grunt or a groan or even fart.

Lonagan thought, *What the hell do I have to do to hurt this guy?*

Night Knuckles drew back his right fist and Lonagan ducked and was grabbed by the throat by a huge ham of a left hand and was lifted kicking straight up off the ground.

While holding him in the air he slammed Lonagan with his right fist in the side of the head.

Lonagan went limp although his legs kicked a few times more.

Grabbing him by the hair of the head with his right hand, Night Knuckles spun Lonagan around. Then he clamped his left arm around Lonagan's neck and put him in a head lock.

Lonagan came back awake and screamed and started punching wildly at any target he could get at. All the targets he could get at were below Night Knuckles waistline.

The referee slapped Night Knuckles on the back and yelled, "Hey! You can't do that. This ain't no rasslin' match!"

Night Knuckles turned a glare on the referee that was so harsh and hard that the referee took three large steps back and said, "Well, I guess since I didn't rightly say that you couldn't do no wrestling, I guess it ain't exactly against the rules."

Night Knuckles gave Lonagan's head a good twist and a loud crack was heard.

Lonagan screamed and yelled, "Oh God, please no!"

Night Knuckles twisted Lonagan's head all the way around backwards with cracks and pops coming from the neck as he did it. Then he just kept on twisting until he'd twisted Lonagan's head around on his shoulders one complete turn and Lonagan's head ripped loose and blood shot up from his stump of a neck as his body collapsed to the ground. Night Knuckles held the head up in front of his face by the hair. He looked into Lonagan's eyes.

Lonagan blinked twice at him. His lips worked up and down like he was trying to form words that he had no air to speak.

The referee stumbled off to the side and kind of mumbled to himself, "Well, I guess there ain't no sense of me counting now is there."

Night Knuckles threw Lonagan's head out into the middle of the crowd.

*   *   *

It took about an hour before all of the side bets on the fight were paid and Dr. Abner collected his winnings for turning Night Knuckles loose on another man.

Then Dr. Abner and Night Knuckles went back to their room at Hillarie's House of Pleasure. There two of Hillarie's finest did their best to fulfill the Doctor's most depraved fantasies while Night Knuckles stood silently watching from a corner.

The girls had no idea that they hadn't even scratched the surface of the depravity that Dr. Abner could sink to.

After two hours of giving it their all the girls were dismissed.

By four AM the torches in the crossroads had burned out and everyone was off the streets of Totem Lake and finally the town seemed to be sleeping.

That was when in the darkness, a shadow darker than the surrounding night, slid down the wall outside the window of the room where Dr. Abner and Night Knuckles stayed.

The shadow slid down the street and vanished into an alley.

The next day a family that lived on the edge of town was found dead in their home. All the blood was drained from their bodies.

CHAPTER TWO

Sometimes a man's gotta do what a man's gotta do and Buck L. Morrison was the kind of man who always did what he needed to do. As he left the Big Oak Tavern in Falling Town Buck L. Morrison realized that what he needed to be doing was making some money.

Morrison was a traveling freelance Bare Knuckle Prize Fighter. He went from town to town and would challenge the biggest and ugliest boys in those towns to fight. Morrison made his money from whatever side bets he could drum up.

Buck L. Morrison was of average height and was slim built. Him, being built slim was what usually gave the local tough guys the confidence to accept his challenge without a moment's hesitation.

The problem was when those big boys started swinging at Morrison they found out that putting a shot on him was as hard as getting a ghost in a headlock. Morrison's boxing style was slick and smooth and he had the fastest hands west of … well, west of anywhere.

Lately though, Morrison had been having a hard time getting any takers to his invitation to a good knuckle dusting. He was traveling a circuit of lumber jack towns and was finding that working lumber jacks traveled around about as much as he did. Word of his arrival started preceding him.

The last two towns Morrison had rolled up into in his covered wagon he got the same reception. When he'd went to the local watering-hole where most likely the drunk wanna-be tough guys would be hanging out, all the lumber jacks glared at him like he had the plague and no one stepped forward to accept his challenge of a five dollar side bet to anyone who could take him in a fair fight.

By the time he showed up in Falling Town, Morrison's money was low and his spirits were getting lower.

Falling Town was just a scattering of a dozen or so wood buildings with some lumber jack tents spread out among them. There weren't really any streets in Falling Town, just a road in and a road out and some businesses and dwellings in between.

When Morrison got to town he did what he usually did and headed straight for the tavern. After going through The Big Oak Tavern's swinging bat wings Morrison went straight to the bar and slapped his palm down to make a loud pop and get everyone's attention.

The drinking lumber jacks turned bleary red eyes on him.

Morrison announced, "I am here to say that I can beat the crap right out of any man in this here town in a bare knuckle fist fight and I have five dollars in my pocket that says that none of you can prove me wrong."

There was a moment of silence.

Then the man standing next to Morrison, a big fat guy with a thick red beard and gnats buzzing around his head farted loudly and said, "That's what I think of you fist fighters."

Morrison glanced out of the corner of his eye just in time to see the man's big right fist come flying toward his head.

As quick as a cat he pivoted and ducked and slid off to the side of the drunken fat man.

The fat man drew back his left fist but was far too slow. Morrison stepped in and sank his own right fist up to the wrist in the fat man's gut.

All the wind whooshed out of the fat man's lungs.

He made a gurgling noise from his mouth, bent over and farted loudly again. Then the fat man made another gurgling sound. This time it didn't come from his mouth and the sound was wet and runny.

That sound was followed by the plopping onto the floor of a sizable amount of diarrhea that slid down the fat man's baggy trouser legs.

"That'll teach you not to try to sucker-punch someone who ain't as drunk as you are," Morrison told him.

The rest of the lumber jacks had a good laugh about Red Beard crapping his pants and Buck L. Morrison was not able to make a cent that night.

After a bit of back slapping from a few of the jacks that couldn't stand the sight of Red Beard, Morrison retreated outside to his covered wagon and got some sleep. It always amazed him how everyone talked about how rough and tough these tree chopping boys were but when it came to meeting a real fighter they just didn't want to know.

*   *   *

The next morning Morrison checked around Falling Town about getting a short term job and making money the way most folks did.

First he went to the livery stable to see if they needed someone to feed and water the horses and clean up around the place. The owner of the livery stable had a son and told Morrison he didn't need a second slave. The one he had worked for free.

Then Morrison went to the Sheriff's office to see if he needed anyone to fix something or maybe just keep a watch on any prisoners he might have.

The Sheriff told him he didn't need anything fixed and he'd be damned if he'd ever arrest anybody for anything. He was just there to pick up a paycheck.

If there was a fight, the Sheriff let them fight it out. If something got stolen, as far as he was concerned they could keep it and if there was a shoot-out he'd make sure he snuck up behind the guy doing the shooting and blast him with his rifle from a long way off.

The only thing the jail was used for was when somebody got too drunk to make it home, he'd let them sleep it off there. If they threw up in the jail, the Sheriff would make them clean the entire jailhouse. Come to think of it, that was the only time the jailhouse got cleaned at all.

The Sheriff didn't need any help and didn't want any.

The last stop on Morrison's round for looking for work was The Big Oak Tavern.

After going up to the bar Morrison asked, "You got some work you need done around here? Right about now, I can be hired fairly cheap."

The bartender looked at Morrison out of the side of his eye as he was wiping glasses clean and said, "You remember that pile of crap that guy left of the floor last night after you hit him in the slats?"

"Yeah I do," Morrison answered. "If that boy would've eaten a solid meal before he started drinking that probably never would have happened."

"That's neither here nor there," the bartender said. "I had to clean up the mess you done caused and let me tell you that was some sure enough stinky shit on that floor, you aught to be paying me, not asking me to pay you."

So as it came to pass Morrison hitched up his covered wagon and drove out of Falling Town hoping to find a better place ahead.

CHAPTER THREE

The one thing we got up here in the Northwest is tall trees, big green tall trees that grow so tall it seems like they could rip the clouds open as they drift past.

Back in 1891 there were a whole lot more of those tall trees around. It seemed like everywhere was forest except for the small spots where men cut the trees down and built towns and cities.

Morrison was driving his wagon down a road not really much wider than a trail and was enjoying the sounds of the birds twittering to each other and watching the squirrels doing their acrobatic jumps from tree to tree and just generally enjoying being in the forest.

Don't get me wrong. Morrison liked city life. He likes women and the company of other men, but being out here in the forest was peaceful. There were times when he wished he didn't have to leave the forest at all.

Back before electric lighting was a common thing, when night time fell, traveling usually came to a sudden halt.

In the movies people are always riding their horses at break neck speeds in the middle of the night. In reality, if you rode a horse fast at night in the country, breaking your neck is exactly what you'd be likely to do. Most of the time you couldn't even see the ground in front of you and a horse couldn't see much better.

That was why when the sun started sliding down the horizon, which Morrison couldn't see anyway because of the trees all around him, he found a small clearing beside the road and pulled his wagon off into it.

After building a camp fire and unhitching his horse and tying him to a tree Morrison settled back in front of the dancing flames and ate some jerked beef and some beans he had stashed inside his wagon.

The night was cool and calm. Hoot Owls called to each other in the distance. He was far enough away from any towns so that Morrison did not have to worry much about being waylaid as he slept.

Morrison chewed on the strips of dried salted beef and ate the spoonfuls of beans and in time his mind drifted.

Before he knew it, Morrison was somewhere else.

*   *   *

He could hear thousands of voices chanting his name as he made his way through a huge crowd to a raised square platform in an enormous auditorium. Rows of bright lights shined down and illuminated the raised ring for all the spectators.

And Morrison didn't know how he knew it, but he knew that the thousands of spectators inside this auditorium were just a fraction of the people who would be watching this contest. He knew that millions of people all across the world would be paying to see this contest and that they would be watching it from their homes.

The announcer spoke his name and that of his opponent and the announcer's voice echoed throughout the large building. It was then that he noticed that he wore padded gloves on his hands. The gloves looked something like large mittens, except that the surface over the striking part of the hand was heavily padded.

He was called to ring center and was there given final instructions by the referee who finished with, "Let's get it on!"

I don't know why you're saying that, Morrison thought. You're not fighting tonight.

The bell rang and Morrison woke up.

He'd fallen asleep while leaning his head back on a large rock and had a kink in his neck. He stood up and stretched. It was still dark and his fire had burned down to just a few flickering flames so he climbed into the back of his wagon undid his bedroll and stretched out to go back to sleep.

The images from the dream were still in his head.

Thousands of people chanting his name, *millions* of people seeing him fight all across the Earth. It was a good dream but he knew those kind of things could never happen.

The Great John L. Sullivan had won his world championship from Jake Killrain before a crowd of less than five thousand and the idea of people all over the world seeing you fight from their homes, well that was just plain ridiculous. But the most ridiculous thing that had come from the dream was the idea that fighting with those pillows on your hands could ever replace good old fashioned bare knuckles.

Those kinds of big mittens are only toys for women and children to play with, thought Morrison. He laughed to himself for having such a wild imagination to even dream such things and went back to sleep.

CHAPTER FOUR
Totem Lake

Sheriff Matt Jackson had never had a morning like this one and he was hoping he wouldn't have another.

It all started with Beth Swanson and her husband Ned beating on the door to his jail house and demanding to be let in yelling bloody murder at the top of their lungs.

The Sheriff had to drag himself out of bed in his small room beside the cells. The abortion of a prize fight the night before made certain that it was a long night for the primary peace keeper in Totem Lake. It took him till nearly 3:30 a.m. to get the streets cleared and quiet.

When Matt finally opened the door to his office with bleary eyes and unshaven face he listened to Beth's story of going out to the Miller's house on the edge of town to practice some Sunday Hymns with Anna and little David.

After knocking on the Miller's door and getting no response, Beth started peeking through the windows and saw the family dead inside the house.

Matt got fully dressed, strapped on his six-shooter and hightailed it over to the Miller place.

With the sun scratching his eyes like an angry bobcat the Sheriff dismounted and walked up to the front door and knocked hoping that this was all some kind of a horrible mistake.

No one answered.

He went around the house shouting the Miller's names, Joe and Anna. He got no answer. The Sheriff wasn't the kind of man to ever peek through a neighbor's window, so he never even thought to do what Mrs. Swanson had done.

It was when he came to the back door that Sheriff Matt Jackson stopped dead in his tracks.

The back door to the Miller house was made of thick heavy wood. It weighed at least eighty or ninety pounds. The back door had been ripped loose from its hinges and thrown a good forty feet away from the house.

Sheriff Matt Jackson was a large thick muscled robust man in his mid-thirties. He was a man who took pride in his physical strength. In fact the last man to have a tussle with him told his buddies about a month after recovering from the beating that Matt was as strong as a country ox and his punches felt like mule kicks. He said, "Unless you got the want to hear your own bones break, you best leave that boy alone."

The Sheriff, as strong as he was, knew that he never could have thrown this door as far as it had been tossed. He couldn't have thrown it half that far.

Matt drew his Remington .45 from his holster and shouted the Miller's names again.

Again, no one answered.

It was only nine in the morning and the cool of the night hadn't burned off yet but the Sheriff could hear the buzzing of flies from within the house. In Washington we don't have a large amount of flying insects but this morning it seemed like every fly in the county had headed on over to the Miller house to see what was happening.

Sheriff Matt Jackson stepped in through the back door of the Miller's home. He stepped into a scene of buzzing madness.

Where he'd entered was a combination kitchen and dining room. A large door led into the main living room of the house. The two bedrooms were off opposite sides of that main room.

From where the Sheriff stood in the kitchen he could see two pairs of arms hanging down from somewhere over the doorway.

He went into the front room and saw that all three members of the Miller family were hanging by their feet from the central support beam of the house.

All three: Anna Miller, Joe Miller and little twelve year old David Miller had their throats and wrists cut.

Flies landed on the wet slices and fed upon the fresh blood. The flies swarmed around the room in such numbers that their buzzing made it hard for Sheriff to hear himself think.

18

Matt Jackson felt vaguely dizzy. He'd seen death before, many times but nothing like this. He wanted to go outside and throw up but resisted the urge.

The Sheriff looked around the room. He didn't know a thing about crime solving. He figured his job was keeping the peace and enforcing the law and that was mainly what he tried to do. This time there was something going on that he was not prepared or trained for but he'd do the best he could anyway.

As he looked around the room the Sheriff saw on the wall a strange symbol. The symbol looked something like a lightning bolt with two balls on each end of it inside a circle. The symbol was drawn in blood.

The bodies were hanging by ropes tied around their ankles and they were a long way up off the floor. The boy and his mother, they could have been hoisted up there by a strong man. But the father of the family, Joe Miller, was a large man, he weighed somewhere around two ten or two twenty. It would have taken at least two men to hoist him up there, or one man of incredible strength.

Matt Jackson's mind flashed for an instant to Night Knuckles twisting off Lonagan's head. Well, he was strong enough, the Sheriff had to admit. But he didn't want to even think about that possibility.

The Sheriff had taken his payoff to allow the fight to happen in the center of the town and when Lonagan had been killed he'd just let it go. After all, Lonagan knew there was always the chance of serious injury in a prize fight even if he'd never dreamed that what happened to him was even possible.

Sheriff Matt Jackson looked around the room and found nothing else unusual except for the symbol in blood on the wall.

When he got ready to leave he looked back for a moment. Something was bothering him. Not something he could see but something that was missing.

He'd stepped outside before he realized what it was and rushed back in to confirm his suspicions.

Underneath the bodies on the floor there were spatters and droplets of blood. The three Miller folk's throats and wrists had been cut.

There should have been a whole lot more blood on the floor but there wasn't. The question spoke in the Sheriff's mind, *where had their blood gone?*

*   *   *

The Undertaker Clive Oubben and his two hired helpers went out to the Miller place and collected the bodies.

Before they took them, out of respect for the dead, Clive had the three Millers wrapped in blankets. The bodies were loaded into the back of an open wagon and taken to the Totem Lake Morgue.

As they were carried in to the morgue to be laid on slabs where they would be prepared for burial while they were still outside in the sun one of David Miller's arms slipped loose and his hand slid out into the sunlight.

No one saw the hand begin to smoke. No one saw the hand shake and tremble then withdraw itself back into the fold inside the blankets, back inside the sheltering darkness.

CHAPTER FIVE

The next morning before he hitched up the horse and started out again Morrison tried his hand at hunting rabbits and squirrels. He had a good supply of jerked beef and beans but after three straight meals of that stuff he was starting to have the kind of gas that would make a party of Sioux Warriors run the other direction.

Morrison had a Colt 44 Revolver that he wore on his hip but pistols weren't any good for hunting anything other than people so he dug out his Winchester 30-30 and headed out into the brush.

The brush was thick and the squirrels were plentiful but after Morrison missed his first shot all the squirrels vanished. He tramped around after that looking for rabbits and never saw a one.

He guessed that they were a little too smart to be hanging around after he missed that first shot.

After stumbling around for awhile and getting all scratched up by the bramble bushes, Morrison headed back to his wagon. He promised himself at the next town he'd trade in the rifle for a shotgun. If he ever got in this situation again he figured he might actually be able to hit something if he was pointing a shotgun at it.

Morrison hitched up the wagon and headed on down the trail in front of him, not quite knowing exactly where he was going, but knowing that this road would lead him to another town.

As he came around a bend Morrison came to an unusual sight. Just off the road two young guys, either in their late teens or early twenties were cussing and poking a stick at an Indian woman they had backed up against a thick black berry bush.

Morrison reared his horse to a stop and watched for a moment. He could tell that the Indian woman was attractive despite the layer of dirt she wore.

Everybody out in the country usually were kind of grimy so a little bit of filth didn't put him off one bit. In fact Buck L. Morrison was far past needing a bath himself. Lately that had been one luxury he just couldn't afford.

The two guys were cussing at the woman and she was snarling and hissing back at them like an angry lizard and shouting something at the boys in her native language.

Morrison climbed down from his wagon and yelled at the boys, "Why y'all got to be bothering this woman? I don't see how she could be hurting you."

"We're just having some fun mister," the larger of the two guys yelled back. "Hell, she's an injun! It ain't like she's a real woman anyway."

Morrison could see from the Indian woman's face expression that she understood what the boy said and it stung her. Even if the woman chose to not speak English, she sure understood it.

"So she ain't done nothing to you?" Morrison asked.

"We found her here," the smaller guy said and now Morrison noted a family resemblance between the two. They were probably brothers, he decided. "She was sleeping and we decided to have some fun."

"Just like poking a frog with a stick," Morrison said.

"Yeah, that's right," The bigger boy said and the both of them hawhawed.

"That does look like fun," Morrison told them walking up. He reached for the stick. "Let me have a little bit of that fun."

The bigger guy had the stick and looked at Morrison to see if he was serious.

"Well come on," Morrison said. "Don't you go hogging all that fun just for yourself, let me see that stick."

The young guy laughed and handed the stick over.

Morrison glanced at the Indian woman. She had anger in her eyes for him. He smiled at her.

He turned back to the two guys. "Well I do have to disagree with you about her not being a real woman," Morrison told them. "And you are two of the dumbest stumps I have ever run across."

"What?" the bigger guy said and Morrison brought the stick around in a wide arcing swing that whopped him on the side of the head and knocked him to his back in the dirt.

Morrison winked at the Indian woman who was now smiling back at him.

He said to the brothers, "Why I do believe swinging this here stick sure is some good fun."

"You can't do that," the smaller brother yelled.

"Sure I can," he answered and jumped at him and gave him a good whack.

The whack landed on the young guys back since he was turning away and starting to run.

He yelled, "Ow!" and took off. The boy had some quick feet too.

When the other brother got to his feet, Morrison chased the two of them out into the road then down it a piece yelling at them, "Get your hides back home you no account varmints. Tell your momma and daddy to teach you some manners."

The brothers took off running into the woods and the last thing he heard from them was when they shouted back, "We'll tell our uncle what you did. He's a champion fist fighter from the East. He'll beat the tar out of you."

Morrison shouted after them, "Good! Tell him we'll fight for a side bet. I charge money for raising knots."

* * *

Back at his wagon the Indian woman thanked Morrison for dealing with the two brothers. She spoke good English with only a slight Indian accent.

"That was nothing," Morrison told her. "They're just a couple of young-sters that don't know their butts from mud puddles."

Morrison climbed back up in his wagon and said, "Well I guess I'll be moving along. You shouldn't have any more problems with those two."

"Can I have a ride with you?" The Indian woman asked.

"Well I'd like to," Morrison told her. "But I'm a single man and I always travel alone. That's just the way I am. I hope you understand." He flicked the reins and drove his wagon on down the road thinking maybe I should learn how to play the guitar someday. That would have made some good words for a song.

So he rolled on down the wagon trail trying to sing a song out of the lyrics, *"I hope you understand, that's just the way I am, I'm a single traveling man."*

He sang so loud that he didn't notice when the Indian woman ran up behind the wagon and smoothly hoisted herself up and inside and laid down and got comfortable for the ride.

CHAPTER SIX
Totem Lake

Word of the murder of the Miller family spread fast and an angry crowd had gathered outside the Jail House by noon. This wasn't just a group of angry people outside the Sheriff's front door. This was a crowd that wanted blood. This was a lynch mob.

The problem was … there was no one to lynch.

The Sheriff with his Deputy, Dan Carson, went out to talk to the mob.

A man in front of the mob that the Sheriff recognized as the town's normally mild mannered banker, Robert English, shouted to Matt as he came out the door, "We want the killer! The Miller's were our neighbors and friends and somebody's got to pay for their deaths."

"I agree," the Sheriff shouted back. "But we got to figure out who did it first. Right now we got no suspects."

That quieted them for a moment so the Sheriff went on. "When I find out who did the crime, we'll have a trial then hang the bastards."

"Sounds like you think it was more than one," Robert English shouted back.

"I don't see how it could have been done by only one man," The Sheriff said. Then he added, "We got some kind of a maniac loose around town. If I had a family, I'd make sure I knew where they were and I'd be guarding them with a gun. So you all head on home. Protect your families and leave me to find out who killed the Millers."

The crowd made some grumbling noises but the Sheriff and his Deputy were happy to see it when the mob started breaking up.

When the crowd dispersed the one man that was left standing in the street outside the Jail House was a small man dressed all in black, Dr. Abner.

He walked up to the Jail House and ascended the three wooden steps.

"We need to talk Sheriff," he said.

Matt Jackson answered, "I don't have time for you right now."

Dr. Abner looked deep within the Sheriff's eyes. His were the kind of eyes that when they were directed at you, they caught your gaze and you could not look away.

Fleetingly the Sheriff remembered the first time he'd seen Dr. Abner.

Abner drove into town in what looked like a large wooden box on wheels drawn behind two black horses. The small traveling home was painted in the garish colors of reds, blues, yellows and greens.

"PROFESSIONAL BARE KNUCKLE FIST FIGHTER" was emblazoned on the side and a poster sized picture of Night Knuckles in a fighting pose was below that.

Dr. Abner parked outside the Jail House and walked in to meet the Sheriff.

After shaking his hand, which Matt Jackson found icy to the touch, the Sheriff told Abner immediately, "No prizefights are allowed in this town. We're peace loving folks. We don't need no shows like that."

Dr. Abner looked in his eyes then, just like he was looking now and the Sheriff found himself saying, "For a licensing fee of fifteen dollars you can hold your contest in town center."

He didn't know why he had done a complete turnaround. He just knew that he had.

Then Sheriff Matt Jackson had spilled forth the information about who the most noted fighter in the territory was. At that time, that fighter had been Lonagan.

He even sent over his Deputy with the hand written challenge to Lonagan. The rest, as it is said, is now history.

Dr. Abner was now looking into his eyes the same way he had looked into them on that day.

Abner spoke. "We need to move on up the ladder. We need international acclaim. Who do you know in this territory who has fought fighters of international fame?"

The Sheriff did not want to answer. He did not want another blood bath of a prize fight to happen in his town.

He opened his mouth to say this and out came, "Jake Killrain once fought John L. Sullivan in a losing effort for the World Bare Knuckle Championship. If Night Knuckles fights and beats him, his reputation would be made. That would make him a legitimate challenger to John L. Sullivan himself."

"And where might I find this Jake Killrain?" Dr. Abner asked.

"A county over to the south; I hear Killrain is out there visiting some relatives."

"Thank you," Dr. Abner told Sheriff Matt Jackson. "I'll reward you for this information when the time is right."

Abner turned to leave and the Sheriff realized that they were inside the Jail House and alone. His Deputy was gone. He didn't know where to. He couldn't remember walking back inside but here he was sitting at his desk.

Matt Jackson felt like he was half asleep. He shook his head to clear the cobwebs out of his mind.

When Dr. Abner reached for the door handle he stopped and turned and again locked eyes with the Sheriff.

"By the way," Dr. Abner said. "This murder thing at the Miller's place, it is not important. Do not spend much effort on trying to solve it. Do you hear what I say?"

"I hear what you say," The Sheriff said. "It is not important."

"Good," Dr. Abner said. He smiled and left.

CHAPTER SEVEN

Buck L. Morrison drove his covered wagon down the trail and the day went by slowly. First, he came to the end of that stretch of forest not far from where he'd stopped the boys from poking at the Indian woman.

At the edge of the woods a smaller wagon trail ran up into the countryside. That road went off into the misty distance and a farm house could be seen on the other side of a few grassy fields with cattle grazing in them.

The two brothers were walking away down that smaller trail in the direction of the farm house.

Morrison couldn't stop himself. It was too tempting. He stood up and shouted at the youngsters, "Y'all get on home to Momma before I get down from this wagon and whip you with that stick again!" Then he laughed. It was a hearty laugh, the kind of laugh that a man has when he enjoys life no matter what it throws at him.

Both of the brothers made obscene hand gestures back at Morrison and that made him laugh some more.

"That's good boys," Morrison shouted after them. "You know where you can shove those fingers too."

After riding the wagon for another few hours Morrison came to another patch of forest. He decided he was getting hungry and pulled off the side of the trail and went into the back of his wagon and the Indian woman yelled out in surprise.

She startled Morrison so he shouted, "Hey, what the hell are you doing back here?"

Shingi wiped the sleep from her eyes. "I took a ride," she told him.

"I thought I told you I don't give rides," Morrison said.

"Yes you did," Shingi answered. "So I did not ask again. I needed it, so I took the ride."

Morrison dug out his supply of jerked beef and Shingi got down from the wagon and went and sat on a large rock.

Morrison came out of the wagon and went over to Shingi.

"It wouldn't be very neighborly of me if I didn't offer you some of this here beef," he said and held out a piece of the dried meat.

Shingi took the beef in her hand. She looked at it, sniffed it and wrinkled up her nose. "I would rather eat old moccasins," she told him.

"Well ain't you something," Morrison told her. "You come asking me for a free ride then won't take any food when it's offered."

"I do not want a free ride," Shingi told him, "And I won't eat bad food when good food is all around us."

"You mean like those critters," Morrison said motioning to some squirrels in low hanging branches. "I spent all morning trying to get me one of those. Didn't have any luck."

"I can catch them," Shingi said.

Morrison laughed. "What you gonna do, hit one with a rock?"

Then he watched as the Indian woman stood up and looked around the ground for a few minutes. Then Shingi bent down and picked up a good sized rock. She hefted it a few times testing its weight.

The Indian woman walked toward the tree where the squirrels played. She spoke something to them in her native language that sounded soft and soothing.

The squirrels stopped their playing and seemed to look in her direction.

Shingi stepped forward and whipped her arm backwards in a wide overhead arc that stopped below her waist and let fly with a stone from there.

The rock flew true and struck the squirrel nearest her in the head. He toppled from the tree to the ground.

Shingi calmly walked over to the stunned animal speaking soothing words as she came. Then she picked up the squirrel and rubbed its head in a caressing fashion and quickly snapped its neck.

*   *   *

As they cleaned the squirrel Morrison asked the Indian woman what she had been saying to the squirrel just before she hit him with the rock.

"I was talking to him and to my gods," Shingi told Morrison. "First I asked my gods if they would let this small animal come back as a mighty hawk in his next life. They told me that they would. I told this to the squirrel and he let me take him so he could move on to the better life that comes next."

"I may not know exactly what you're talking about," Morrison told her. "But it worked good enough for me."

After a meal of cooked squirrel meat Morrison decided they should stay exactly where they were for the night. A stomach full of good food will do that for a man.

After Morrison had settled back by the fire to get comfortable Shingi went over and petted his horse's head and talked to him. The horse was a beautiful white and brown paint mustang.

She asked Morrison, "What is his name?"

Morrison answered, "Well, I just call him Horse now. It started out something different. I can't remember what I originally called him but as it turned out about half the time I was saying, what's wrong with you, you stupid horse or you idiot horse why'd you have to take a crap in the camp fire or something like that. After a while he was just Horse to me."

"What's your name?" Morrison asked her.

"I am of the What-the-hey tribe," The Indian woman said. "I am called Shingi Notowatakanay Whowhatokanangi."

"You don't say," Morrison told her. "I think I'll just start right off the bat and call you Woman. What-the-hey, Woman?" He said and laughed.

Shingi just shook her head. She couldn't believe these people had actually taken over her country.

CHAPTER EIGHT

The sun went down behind the hills and the moon came out and Shingi stretched out in the back of the wagon and rested although she was a long way from being sleepy. Morrison had taken out his bed roll and hunkered down next to the fire. He told Shingi she could sleep inside the wagon.

Shingi was even more used to sleeping out in the open underneath the stars than Morrison was. But she knew he was being nice to her so she took him up on his offer of shelter.

She lay in the semi-darkness of the wagon and listened to the sounds of the fire crackling, bull frogs croaking, and night birds calling to each other. All these sounds were like music to her ears. This was the land she had known since birth.

The land was alive, this she knew. It was changing but living things always change. Whether the changes were for the better or for the worse she could not be the judge.

That was only for the Gods to decide.

She lay there in the semi-darkness and listened. One thing in particular is what she listened for. She listened for Morrison's breathing to become regular, to have the steady rhythm of sleep.

It took a long while and she almost fell asleep herself waiting but finally Shingi did begin to hear the steady in and out of his breath.

Shingi waited a few minutes more and the breathing got louder until it sounded like someone was using a large saw on a tree.

Morrison was most definitely asleep she decided, even if probably nothing else in the forest was.

She climbed out of the wagon and stood before the fire.

Raising her hands over her head Shingi chanted an ancient song that was soothing to the ears and all the creatures around the campsite, except for Morrison, went silent.

The Indian Medicine Woman sent her mind out over the vast distances between this world and the world of the spirits. Shingi felt herself, her spirit fly, the wind swooshing through her hair. She was moving at an incredible speed until all at once, she felt herself stop.

All around Shingi was darkness. In the far distance stars twinkled but even they seemed like far away weak points of light. She floated in an empty black sky, weightless, bodiless, totally alone.

She was not afraid.

She had come to this place many times.

She called out to the Great Spirit of the Earth with her mind. *I seek your guidance. I know I am to go to a white man's town and stop something terrible from happening. But I do not know where that town is. Please, show me the way.*

Out of everywhere around her and out of nowhere, a voice came to Shingi. The voice was strong. It spoke.

"Follow the man," it said. "Where he goes the darkness awaits. The darkness that you must battle grows strong upon fear. It grows strong upon the blood of the murdered. It is ancient and cannot be allowed to continue."

"Will the man help me fight the darkness?" Shingi asked.

The voice answered, "Your two destinies are now one. Watch and you will know."

Before Shingi a scene unfolded of grey stone walls and many children packed into a large building. She was seeing the inside of an orphanage that she somehow knew was in the white man's city of St. Louis.

The sleeping rooms were over crowded. The meals that the children were given were never enough, but the nuns who raised them did the best that they could.

Every day the children were taught the rudiments of reading, writing and arithmetic in one large school room. They tried to teach the children such things as manners and how to conduct themselves in public but accepted that most of those lessons were ignored.

One nun named Sister Jane Wently tried very hard to instill in the young boys a code of conduct and a sense of right and wrong. She did this by having them read the stories of King Arthur and the Knights of the Round Table.

The stories were exciting adventures that put forth the virtues of doing good deeds and chivalry. Most of the kids laughed it off as stupid fantasies that had no place in the real world.

One little boy did not.

That little boy was Buckley L. Morrison. He loved the idea that the strong should look out for and care about the weak. He wanted to do great things with his life. Things like helping people in trouble.

Sister Jane told him he would have to wait until he was grown then someday he would find a quest for the good that he could call his own and when he did he would know it.

The little boy was a battler too. He wasn't big but he was extremely fast. When the older, larger boys picked on him they quickly learned to regret it.

One day in an effort to instill in the boys a sense of self-discipline the Sisters invited an instructor in the art of pugilism or Bare-Knuckle Fist Fighting to come and speak to them.

The instructor was Professor Mike O' Dowd, a man of medium height with a strong build and a cultured unmarked face. He took the boys out into the large open courtyard of the orphanage and first explained who he was.

In a time when Bare-Knuckle Prize Fighting was illegal in most of the United States, O'Dowd was a master at unarmed combat. He made the majority of his living teaching affluent gentlemen what they should do if they were accosted by street toughs.

O'Dowd started off by showing the boys the proper way to stand and hold their hands to have a good defense and be balanced to counter attack. Some listened. Most did not.

After that he showed the boys how to throw jabs and short hooks and short compact crosses. By now most of the boys were bored with his talking and wanted to move onto something different.

One little boy who was thirteen years old was paying very close attention. That thirteen year old was Buckley L. Morrison. He was even doing an expert imitation of the blows O'Dowd was demonstrating off to the side and out of his sight.

When the demonstration was done O'Dowd called for some volunteers so he could show how the techniques he demonstrated worked during actual combat.

"I need at least two of you to step forward for advanced instruction," O'Dowd told the youths. "I promise not to hurt you and you'll learn plenty before I am through."

Buckley L. Morrison threw his hand up and stepped forward. He was told to go back. O'Dowd wanted a few of the largest boys to show the value of brain over brawn.

None of the larger boys stepped forward so O'Dowd picked the two largest ones.

O'Dowd told the largest youth, a big bruiser by the name of Timmy Sears to attack him.

With a yell that any Indian War Chief would have been proud of Sears charged O' Dowd with his right fist raised above his head like it was a rock he was going to slam down upon the head of a bull whose skull he was going to crush.

O'Dowd caught Sears's fist with his open left hand and directed it past him and at the same time stepped to the side and delivered a stinging backhand slap to Sears that sent him sliding in the dirt on his face.

The next boy did not charge in wild when beckoned to do so. O'Dowd had to go to him. O'Dowd threw a fake jab at the boy's face and when the boy threw both hands up to block the jab, O'Dowd foot swept him and gave him a straight arm shove depositing him on his butt in the dirt.

"And so that concludes our lesson," O'Dowd told the boys and told them to go back to their class where the nuns awaited.

"You haven't given me a try," Buckley L. Morrison shouted at him as he turned to go.

"Sorry son," O'Dowd told him. "You're too small for me to demonstrate on. Maybe we'll do it in a few years."

"Maybe you're too afraid to?" Morrison asked him.

There was laughter that came from the boys still milling around in the courtyard.

O'Dowd was being showed up and he knew it. *Why you cheeky little bastard, he thought. I guess I will have to teach you a lesson.*

"All right," O'Dowd told him. "I'll try not to hurt you." He stepped forward. "Show me what you've learned."

O'Dowd was an average sized man in good physical shape, measuring up against the thirteen year old Buckley L. Morrison he looked like a giant. He didn't want to hurt the kid but he did want to get this over with as quick as possible. He'd spent more time at this orphanage this afternoon than he'd planned on and he had a paying engagement to go to.

O'Dowd stepped forward and threw an open left hand slap at Morrison either expecting him to throw both hands up or to simply run away from the blow.

What he got, was that Morrison slipped under the punch by bending at the knees, stepped forward and a little to his own right and dug a good short left uppercut to O'Dowd's kidney.

The punch hurt like hell.

It wasn't hard because the boy was only thirteen, but the placement of the blow lanced a jolt of pain into O'Dowd's side.

O'Dowd stepped back and chuckled. "Good shot boy," He said. "Everybody gets lucky some time."

He stepped forward and threw a right cross with his doubled up fist. No way was he going to let some snot nosed kid get the better of him, not in front of a yard full of hooting youngsters he wasn't.

Morrison slapped the punch to the side with his open left just like he'd seen O'Dowd demonstrate and stepped in with a short straight right of his own to the point of O'Dowd's chin.

Stars exploded inside O'Dowd's head. He grabbed Morrison and pulled him in close in a bear hug.

"You little fucking bastard," He yelled when his senses came all the way back.

He picked Morrison up and threw him to the ground knocking the wind out of him. Then O'Dowd jumped on Morrison and started punching wildly. But even from the ground Morrison rolled and tucked his legs in sliding away and slipped the blows.

"Mr. O'Dowd! What are you doing?" One of the nuns shouted and O'Dowd realized how bad this must look.

"What is the matter with you?" The nun yelled. "You were trying to hurt that boy."

"I was just playing around a bit," O'Dowd told the nun but he could barely get the words out because he was breathing so hard.

O'Dowd turned to leave.

Morrison shouted, "Where are you going? We ain't done yet. We ain't done by a long shot!"

And Shingi found herself back in front of the campfire that Morrison slept beside.

She looked down at Morrison and thought, *I'm glad you are on my side,* because she knew that the kind of man that he was, was the kind that never gave up. If he was outsized, outgunned or outnumbered it wouldn't matter.

Once he started to fight Buckley L. Morrison would never give up until the bloody end.

CHAPTER NINE
Totem Lake

Night came to the Town of Totem Lake like a black panther on the prowl, silent and lethal.

Sheriff Matt Jackson made his rounds in what looked almost like a ghost town. It was still pretty early but all of the businesses except for Hillarie's House of Pleasure and Charley's Saloon were closed. Except for a few horses tied up outside Charley's the streets were deserted.

A few candles burned in windows to show that there was life within those buildings but that was it.

Tension hung heavy in the air. The murders of the Miller family had everyone on edge.

The Sheriff made his rounds and everything seemed calm and quiet, too calm and quiet. It felt like a calming of the wind before a tornado.

He walked down the street checking the businesses and for once he could hear the crunch of his own boots in the dirt. He could hear his own breathing.

Totem Lake was not normally a wild place to be when the sun went down but usually there were the sounds of guys laughing a little too loud from the saloon or the sound of a drunk stumbling over his own two feet and vomiting in the middle of the street.

Tonight, none of that was happening.

In a strange way the Sheriff missed it. At least when things like that went on, it showed that the town was alive.

Tonight, silence hung in the air like an executioner's ax.

Sheriff Matt Jackson finished his rounds. He went into the jail house and sat down behind his desk. In the left top side drawer there was a pint of whiskey.

He pulled it out, uncorked the bottle and took a large swallow.

The liquid burned as it went down. It brought tears to his eyes.

The whiskey was rot gut, the cheapest he could get hold of in a large quantity.

He carried the bottle to his small room beside the jail cells and sat down on his bed.

The Sheriff took another big slug.

Sleep would come hard tonight, but this would help.

*   *   *

Jeremy Slater and Carl Howard watched the Sheriff as he did his rounds from the shadows of the alley between Johnson's Finest Tobaccos and Wesley's Gunsmith Shop. Tonight was just the kind of night these two had been waiting for.

They crept around back of the Gunsmith Shop and Jeremy produced a long bar of steel that had been beaten down to a tapering flat edge at one end.

The darkness hung heavy in the air. The silence was oppressive.

Carl kept watch at the edge of the building. From where he was he could see both the back of the Blacksmith Shop and the Jail House. He was there to keep watch to make sure the Sheriff did not come out after he closed up for the night.

Jeremy went to work on the door. He worked as quietly as he could. That was the one drawback of just about everyone being at home scared in their beds. Jeremy felt like it was so quiet that if he made any noise at all, someone had to hear.

Carl shushed him from the corner of the building and Jeremy froze.

The Sheriff had stuck his head in the window for one last look-see. As soon as he disappeared back inside the room the lantern was extinguished and the Jail House went completely dark.

Carl whispered to Jeremy to get back to work on that door.

With visions of the money they'd make from selling stolen guns dancing in his head Jeremy did exactly that.

He managed to wedge his pry bar into the door just the way he wanted to and there was only the small sound of wood splintering like a piece of paper being ripped when he forced the wood away from the latch. Then he stood in front of the open door.

Jeremy sensed more than saw a huge black shape rise up beside him. His first thought was that for some strange reason Carl had abandoned his lookout. But Carl would have been on his other side.

He said, "Wha…"

And the air was cut off from his lungs by a claw-like hand that grabbed him around the throat and lifted him above the ground, his feet kicking the air.

The hand tightened ... closed ... the bones of Jeremy Slater's throat were crushed and snapped like small twigs used to start a campfire.

He was tossed to the side like discarded trash.

From the corner of the building Carl asked back over his shoulder, "Did you say something?"

He glanced over his shoulder and saw the shape approaching him.

"Boy you best get back in there and get them dam guns," Carl whisper-shouted.

It was the last words he would ever say.

*   *   *

Rhonda Baskins stumbled out the front door of Hillarie's House of Pleasure helped along by a healthy shove by the Madam herself.

"And stay gone!" Hillarie shouted after her, "Until you learn to keep a civil tongue in your head and learn how to treat a paying customer."

"Well, bloody-hell, I couldn't help me-self," Rhonda shouted back at the brothel owner. "What with the Reverend preaching at me how he was going to teach me to be a good girl with his staff of God and all. Then he drops his drawers and all he's got is a little limp noodle.

"I'm sorry! It was hilarious. I couldn't stop me-self from laughing," Rhonda said.

The door was slammed in her face.

Oh, sod it all, she thought. Rhonda was new to the territory. She'd taken the boat over from Ireland after hearing about the mythical streets of gold in America.

She'd not found any streets of gold or any gold at all for that matter. All that Rhonda had found since she came to the west was a lot of horny cowboys and farmers and tonight the local preacher.

Well, she knew how her fortune was to be made, but for tonight she just needed to find a place to sleep.

She walked down the street feeling the cool night air, thinking that it was quiet out and that the air had the feel of rain in it. Rhonda headed toward Charley's Saloon. That was the most likely spot for finding a companion for the night.

Actually, she could care less about a companion. She just wanted a warm bed and a roof over her head.

Rhonda walked past two businesses. Then she saw him there standing back in the dark. She saw his eyes glisten.

One's just as good as another, she thought and walked toward the alley. She flipped her reddish blond hair with a shake of her head so that its color caught the moonlight.

"Hey mister," Rhonda called in her sexiest little girl voice. "Do you think you might need some company tonight?"

She was close to the alley now and he was coming out of the shadows.

He was a large man, weighed roughly around two ten. His face was so clean he looked down right pale in the moonlight. He reached his hands out and she went to him and saw to her horror as he stepped completely out of the shadows and into the white light of the moon that he had been ripped open from chest to beltline and he was hollow inside.

Rhonda went to scream and the thing grabbed her and dragged her to him for a hellish embrace. He forced his hand over her mouth and cut off her cries.

Rhonda was dragged back into the darkness of the alley.

*   *   *

Enrique Sanchez was still fuming at his wife Maria as he left Charley's Saloon and climbed onto old Bess his brown and white paint pony. They had a farm about a mile out of town and he'd worked hard all day long, just like he worked every day, milking the cows, feeding the chickens, plowing the fields and doing everything that a good man should do.

Then when he'd gotten home the first thing he'd done was thrown his arms around his wife for a big fat kiss and all he got was a shove away and a, "Oh don't you put your hands on me. You smell! You are a stinky man."

He countered with, "Of course I'm a stinky man. Who you think does the work around here?"

That opened the flood gates. Maria wanted a baby. Enrique wanted to wait till they were better off and how in the hell were they going to get a baby anyway if she wouldn't let him touch her.

It went back and forth like that for a while until Enrique slammed the door shut behind him and rode into town and had a few beers.

The beers had not calmed him down. In fact it seemed like they had done the opposite. It was like the alcohol was being poured on a fire. He was still angry but now he was more than slightly drunk.

Enrique rode down the street rehearsing his speech in his mind. *Look Maria, he'd say. I'm a man. I give you a good home. I don't beat you. God knows I've been tempted. I don't yell, well not very much anyway. I try. Really, I do. You got to try now too girl. I give, so for us to be happy you need to give some too.*

He was wrapped up in his internal dialogue, running this speech over in his mind when he reached the edge of town and as he passed the edge of the last building he saw something move fast back in the blackness.

A weight struck him on the back as something leaped up into the air and grabbed him around the neck and bore him to the ground.

Enrique had the air knocked out of him but did not think about that. He punched out blindly and his fist connected on solid flesh. The thing rolled away from him.

Enrique got to his knees and sucked in a heaving lungful of air.

The thing stood up now and in the moonlight Enrique saw that it was that woman from the church that his wife liked so much, Anna Miller.

"What are you doing?" Enrique asked and at the same time remembered what he'd been told at Charley's about Anna and her entire family being butchered.

Anna leaped on him again knocking him to his back, coming down on his chest with her knees. She looked down on Enrique from where she kneeled on his chest as he fought to regain his breath again and Anna smiled.

Her smile was jagged and pointy.

*   *   *

Beth Swanson was having a hard time falling asleep. Today had been a terrible day. First, she found some of the most devout church goers in the community murdered in their home.

That had been awful, truly awful. Such good people they were too, so kindhearted and full of the spirit of Christ. It was a terrible thing to happen.

No doubt it was some wild Indians that wandered through, she told herself.

So she prayed and asked for the souls of her dear departed friends to be delivered unto Jesus. She found comfort in praying.

But that did not stop her from seeing their faces every time she closed her eyes and tried to go to sleep. Her husband Ned had no such problems. Within a minute of going to bed he was snoring like a hibernating grizzly bear.

So Beth got up and went down to the kitchen. She figured she would drink a glass of milk and read her bible until she got so sleepy that the instant she laid down she would drift off.

Beth got the pitcher of milk and poured herself a tall glass and settled herself down beside her favorite reading lamp when she heard a light rapping at the front door.

It was far after nightfall and Beth wondered who could possibly be calling at this time of night. She got up from her chair and took a step toward the bedroom to rouse Ned and then thought, *he works terribly hard and does need his sleep. I should at least see who it is before I awaken him.*

The light rapping came at the front door again. It was a little more insistent this time.

There was a window to the left hand side of the front door. Beth went to the window and peered out.

On the front porch in the moonlight, a child was standing at her door and knocking. She could not see his face but could tell that it was a boy of maybe twelve or thirteen.

She had her thick house coat on over her long night dress so Beth decided there would be no harm in opening the door to see what the child might want.

The caller was knocking again as Beth turned the knob and pulled the door open.

A startled cry stuck in her throat as Beth stumbled backward and tripped and fell to the floor.

I must be dreaming! I've... I've got to be dreaming! The words screamed inside her head as little twelve year old David Miller bounded into Beth's living room and leaped on top of her and tore her throat open with his bared teeth.

As Beth bled her life out onto the floor, David went into the Swanson's kitchen and started looking through their cutlery drawers. He didn't stop searching until he found a meat cleaver.

Then he paid a visit to Mr. Swanson.

43

CHAPTER TEN

Early the next morning Shingi caught a rabbit with a snare it took her ten minutes to construct. She skinned and cleaned the rabbit and thanked its spirit for the food they were being provided. Morrison cooked the rabbit on a spit over the fire as Shingi gathered some wild berries and some other edible plants that he didn't even know existed.

They ate a good breakfast. It was the best breakfast Morrison had eaten in months.

When they set out that day, Shingi sat beside Morrison. She had definitely proven she could carry her own weight and to him that was enough to get her out of the back of the wagon.

*   *   *

Morrison drove the wagon down the trail as grey clouds blew across the sky and covered the sun. These were not storm clouds. No lightning crashed to the ground and no thunder was heard.

These were the kind of clouds that inhabit the skies of Washington at least half of the time. There was nothing unusual about this weather.

It grew slightly colder and started to sprinkle about noon. It was the kind of rain where it felt like somebody was spitting at you from a distance and occasionally would hit the target.

This was Western Washington weather. If you lived there, you better get used to it because that's just the way it is.

Somewhere around three o'clock in the afternoon they came to a small town. The town's name was Stillwell.

The town was mainly just a collection of around fifty, one and two story buildings with one main street and two cross streets.

Morrison and Shingi entered from the south on the main street and as was his habit he drove directly to the only saloon in town, a place named

Black Betty's Brew House. The outside of Black Betty's Brew House was dreary. The paint was old and peeling so bad that the sign was barely readable. Morrison pushed through the bat wings and entered.

The inside of Black Betty's Brew House matched the outside. The owner obviously could have cared less if the place looked like a flea pit because that's exactly what it did look like.

There were five tables. Three of them were occupied with four men each playing cards. One of those men was well dressed in a fancy Dan's suit. The rest of the card players looked like cowboy dead beats.

At the bar were six cowboys who were heavily into their beers.

Just like he always did Morrison walked directly to the bar and slapped his palm down to get everyone's attention.

All the cowboys, the barman, and the Fancy Dan looked his way. Another man, a well-muscled guy with a handlebar mustache, stepped inside the saloon through the bat wings.

Morrison made his announcement, "I am here to say that I can beat the crap right out of any man in this here town in a bare knuckle fist fight and I have five dollars in my pocket that says none of you can prove me wrong."

All the cowpokes, the barman and the Fancy Dan did a strange thing then. They all looked at the man who stepped through the bat wings after Morrison.

The man with the handlebar mustache stood just inside the door and smiled at Morrison.

He said, "I have come here to beat the crap out of you and I reckon I'll do it for free."

Mustache man took a few steps toward Morrison and Morrison held up his hands. "I don't fight for free," he said. "We need to get us some side bets going."

"My name is Jake Killrain," the man told Morrison "You took a stick to my two nephews yesterday and I don't cotton to that one bit."

"The boys deserved it," Morrison said. "They were picking on a woman."

"They were running off a thieving injun'," Killrain hissed his face growing red. "I'd a done the same."

He came at Morrison with his fists doubled up and waving in the air out in front of his face like Morrison had seen a few other professional bare-knuckle fist fighters do.

But before he got close enough for the fists to start flying the Fancy Dan jumped between them. "Woe, hold on hoss!" He shouted with both of his hands in the air to halt the proceedings. "If we're going to have us a fight here, there ain't no reason all of us can't make us a dollar or two. Are you *THE* Jake Killrain, the one that fought John L. Sullivan?"

"That I am," Killrain told him.

The Fancy Dan pointed at one of the cowboys who had been playing cards with him.

"Mike, go round up all the cowhands you can from around town and tell them we're gonna have us a real bare-knuckle prize fight in the stable out in back of my hotel."

He stuck his hand out.

"Pleased to meet you Mr. Killrain, I'm Patrick Barnum and I say never do anything for free that you can get paid for."

They shook hands and Barnum shouted, "In one hour, challenger for the World Bare Knuckle Championship Jake Killrain and," He leaned toward Morrison and whispered, "Who the hell are you anyway?" Morrison told him, "Will meet Buck L. Morrison for the newly created Bare Knuckle Championship of Stillwell. It will be in my stable. Y'all know where that is and a price of one dollar gets you on my property for a first-hand look at a world class bare-knuckle fist fight."

*   *   *

On the way to the stable, seeing that a crowd of at least thirty had gathered before they even left the bar, Morrison told Barnum he wasn't fighting without being paid.

Barnum offered him the five dollars he had originally named in the saloon and Morrison laughed.

"That was before you raised a crowd," Morrison told him. "By the time we get to your stable I figure there'll be at least a hundred people waiting."

Killrain looked at Barnum with a mean expression on his face.

"If you pay him, I best get paid," He said. "Or I'll be knocking the teeth out of your head just as soon as I'm done with him." He indicated Morrison.

Barnum was nothing if not fast on his feet.

He said, "OK, this will be a winner take all match. Half of what I take for charging entrance to my property goes to the winner."

Both fighters agreed to that and Barnum breathed a sigh of relief since there wasn't a good dentist in town and he couldn't afford a trip to Seattle right then to get himself a set of new choppers.

*　　*　　*

When Shingi saw Morrison, Barnum and Killrain leading a crowd down the street she followed them. When they got to the stable the guy Barnum stationed at the gate to charge admittance wouldn't let her in.

"This here show is about to get bloody," the cowpoke hired for a dollar and free admittance told her. "Even if you did have a dollar, which I doubt, you're an Injun and we don't let Injuns sit or stand next to good white folks. And even if you weren't an Injun', you're a woman and ain't no women gonna be in here tonight. When these fists start busting skulls we don't need to have no fainting women folk on our hands."

Morrison saw this happening and walked over to the gate keeper.

"What's the problem?" He asked.

The gate keeper started into his, "We won't let," speech and Morrison took Shingi's hand and pulled her past him.

Before the gate keeper could speak Morrison said, "You say one word and you'll be the first man I put face down in the dirt. Wanna try me?" He gave him a mean glare that shut the gate keeper's yap.

They walked out to the center of the corral.

Four posts were quickly being pounded into the ground and rope had been fetched that was going to be stretched between the posts to create a squared off enclosure.

"I appreciate you coming," Morrison told Shingi. "But I'm not going to have any problem with him." He indicated Killrain who was loosening up and throwing mean looks his way.

"Is it not so that we are now partners?" Shingi asked.

"Well, yeah I guess so," Morrison answered. "At least until you wants to go off on your own."

"Good," Shingi said.

There was a leather pouch that Shingi always wore at her waist tied around her by a leather thong. She untied it and reached inside.

Morrison was now doing his loosening up, shadow boxing and throwing punches into the air. He was deliberately moving much slower than he really could. Morrison didn't want to let Killrain get prepared for what was in store for him.

Shingi pulled from the pouch a small carving of an Indian holding a spear above his head. She handed it to Morrison.

"Put this in your pocket," Shingi said. "It will help give you good luck in battle."

"I don't need no luck little lady," Morrison told her. He held a fist up in front of his face. "This here is my luck."

"Take the charm. Put it in your pocket," Shingi said. "You never know when you might need it. We are partners, honor me this way."

Morrison looked at the wood carving. The workmanship was extraordinary.

"Since it means that much to you, what the hell," he said and slipped it into his pocket. He took off his gun belt and handed that to Shingi for safe keeping, then stripped to the waist when Killrain did.

Then the ring ropes were tied and pulled tight against the solidly driven in posts.

The people pouring into the stable dwindled down then stopped coming in. The crowd appeared to be at least two hundred strong.

The majority were rowdy cowhands but there were sprinkled in among them the odd banker and clerk-type guy and a few that looked like dusty desperados.

Patrick Barnum had everyone get out of the ring except for Morrison and Killrain. Then he shouted at the top of his lungs for everyone to shut up.

When the noise quieted down he announced, "Good citizens of Stillwell Washington, I am pleased to bring to you tonight a contest of skill, daring and raw guts."

"Get on with it," somebody shouted from within the impatient crowd.

Barnum continued as though he heard nothing.

"Meeting here tonight for the Bare Knuckle Championship of Stillwell is none other than the one and only Jake Killrain." There were loud cheers. "And Buck L. Morrison," There was a smattering of boos for the unknown new comer. "And I am acting as referee."

"Come to the mark," Barnum said and drew a line in the dirt with the toe of his shoe.

Morrison and Killrain met at ring center and stared at each other with murder in their eyes.

"I'm gonna knock your teeth out of your skull," Killrain hissed.

"Many have tried," Morrison told him. "I still got enough to eat corn on the cob with."

"Are you both ready?" Barnum asked.

Both nodded and brought up their fists.

"Then fight!" Barnum yelled and quickly stepped back. Morrison immediately stepped to his own left and Killrain jumped straight backwards anticipating that Morrison would lunge in at him with a wild swing.

Well at least you ain't like the idiots I'm used to fighting, Morrison thought. He was accustomed to muscle bound lumber jacks and drunken cowhands trying to rip his head off with the first swing. This was going to be an entirely different proposition.

Killrain came forward saying, "What's the matter? You afraid of me since I'm not some kid you can scare off with a stick?"

"Come on and find out," Morrison told him.

49

Killrain lead with a swinging left that Morrison stepped away from and countered with a straight overhand right.

Killrain grabbed and pulled Morrison close.

Morrison went to tie up Killrain's arms and was head butted on his right cheek so hard it rang his ears. He shoved Killrain away.

The crowd cheered Killrain's head butt.

So that's how it's going to be, Morrison thought. *They're going to let you get away with anything you want to.*

He snapped out two jabs that reddened Killrain's nose.

Killrain threw a good hard leg kick to Morrison's right thigh that landed with a *thwack* and stung like hell.

"Stop that right now," Barnum barked at Killrain. "You know that's against the rules."

"There ain't no rules," Killrain yelled. "You never named London Prize Ring or anything else."

Barnum glanced at Morrison.

"That's fine with me," Morrison said. "He's as crooked as a barrel of snakes anyway. If you named some rules, you'd only give him an excuse to break-em." Morrison stepped in with a wide left hook. Killrain saw it coming and ducked.

It was only a feint anyway so what he ducked into was a knee to the teeth.

Killrain's legs folded underneath him and as he went down Morrison caught him with a quick right uppercut.

He drew back his left foot to kick the downed Killrain but held it and yelled at him instead, "Take you're dam thirty seconds rest. You might be a low-down conniving dog but I'm not. I don't kick a man when he's down."

Morrison went over and stood next to Shingi in a corner never taking his eyes off Killrain. The way Killrain was acting he half expected him to pull a gun out of a pocket and start shooting.

Barnum looked at his watch and counted out thirty seconds then he called the two fighters to the mark at ring center.

When he yelled, "Fight!" this time Killrain had a different attitude. He advanced behind a pawing jab and whenever they got in close he grabbed and clutched and didn't try the dirty tactics. Killrain had been woken up rather quickly to the fact that he was in with a fighter of equal of better skill than he had.

The fight became a grueling contest after that initial exchange of punches with Killrain trying every defensive tactic that he knew or had ever even heard of. Several times he went down from what was not actually a punch but only to get the thirty-second rest.

Morrison did the pursuing. He was not used to fighting a man who tried to think about what he did before he did it. For him this was a feel-your-way-through-it type of contest. He made sure that he didn't just wade in throwing wide punches because he was certain that was exactly what Killrain wanted him to do.

So Morrison bided his time and conserved his energy and after about an hour and a half into the contest Killrain made a fatal mistake. It was a very basic mistake brought on as much by mental fatigue as by physical exhaustion.

After one of the hundreds of clinches that Killrain initiated he stepped straight back with both hands at chest level.

Morrison no sooner had seen the opening than he let fly with a left hook-right cross combination that put Killrain on his back in the dirt.

He went down with a thud. Dust flew up from where he struck the ground flat on his back.

This was not one of Killrain's fake knock downs. He was out before he hit the ground.

CHAPTER ELEVEN
Totem Lake

Dr. Abner watched the Town of Totem Lake. He watched everything from his hotel room in Hillarie's House of Pleasure.

The shades were drawn. All the lights were out except for the one candle that burned in the center of the floor.

Dr. Abner sat on the floor cross legged, arms folded over his chest and eyes closed. He had sat this way for a half hour just before dawn sinking deeply within himself. Dr. Abner sank so deep into the darkness within that he could see other worlds inside his own mind, entire universes that he could command.

Then when he was totally separated from the world outside but still in total command of his consciousness, he stepped out, outside of himself.

Dawn was rising when Abner floated above the streets of Totem Lake. The horizon to the east was briefly a fiery blood red with the rising of the sun.

Dr. Abner watched Totem Lake.

First he saw the broken and drained bodies of the two thieves outside the back door of Wesley's Gunsmith Shop. The twisted bodies lay out in the open, still as death, until the first rays of sunlight touched them. Then a smoke started coming from their skin like a wet log laid on a fire that hasn't yet caught.

With the smoke their limbs started jerking and both thieves rolled over onto their stomachs. The sun scorched the bare skin on the backs of their hands and the back of their necks. With the rising of the smoke they came alive.

Like cockroaches suddenly discovered they scurried away toward the dark in the crawlspace under the floor of Wesley's Gunsmith Shop.

When they found a spot beneath the center of the flooring far away from where the light could reach them they stopped moving and waited for nightfall.

Dr. Abner watched as Rhonda Baskins lying in the alley with her throat ripped open began to smoke with the coming sun. He watched as she dug herself a furrow beneath a large mound of the trash and garbage that had accumulated in the alley. Rhonda buried herself beneath the pile then moved no more.

Enrique Sanchez dug himself into the dirt with his bare fingers and Mr. and Mrs. Swanson slept the day away beneath their queen sized bed.

Dr. Abner watched all of this and smiled. All of his children of the night found shelter from the burning sun. All was going according to plan.

This town, this small place was but a dress rehearsal for the eventual main event.

Eventually, John L. Sullivan, the World Heavyweight Bare Knuckle Champion and Boston waited.

For now Totem Lake would be his.

*   *   *

A pounding came at the door of the Jail House and Sheriff Matt Jackson stumbled out of bed. He knocked his bottle of rot-gut whiskey off the side table and watched as it gurgled out onto the floor.

Through the window shades the sun scorched his eyes. *This being woke up early in the morning was getting to be a bad habit.*

The pounding on the door came again.

The Sheriff yelled as loud as he could, "I'll be there in a god-dammed minute and this better be good or you'll be spending the day locked up."

He regretted yelling the moment he did it. His head felt like it was splitting open.

"God-dammed cheap whiskey," he muttered and snatched up what was left of the bottle from the floor.

Only a single drink was left and he slugged that down. It didn't help. The whiskey only made him feel like throwing up.

He didn't.

The Sheriff got dressed and went to the door and threw it open. The little skinny guy with wire rimmed spectacles who owned the gun smith shop was there.

"Sheriff, I've been broken into," Wesley said sounding out of breath.

Matt Jackson grabbed his gun-belt off the wall and buckled it on.

"Was anything taken?" He asked.

"I-I don't know," Wesley said. "I haven't gone in yet. Wha-what if they are still there?"

"Hell, with all the guns you got," the Sheriff told Wesley, "I'd have figured you'd just charge right in there and fill-em full of lead."

The look on Wesley's face told the Sheriff that while Wesley had a love of firearms he just wasn't the type to ever use one.

"Well, lead the way then," Matt Jackson said. "We'll find out what happened."

In back of his shop Wesley showed the Sheriff where his door had been pried open. Matt Jackson drew his six-shooter and stood off to the side of the door. He was hoping he wouldn't have to do any shooting until at least in the afternoon.

With a hangover like this one if a bandit didn't get him, the sound of his own gun firing would probably kill him.

Matt shouted, "If you're in there you'd best give up. We've got the place surrounded." The Sheriff knew that sounded stupid but it sounded like lawman talk and it was expected of him.

He also knew that the place was empty. No thief would wait around all morning for you just to come and get him.

When no answer came the Sheriff stepped inside and lo and behold there were no bandits.

But what surprised him was when Wesley checked out his shop and nothing was missing.

What the hell was going on here? The Sheriff asked himself and as he walked away he saw the dried blood on the ground outside the back door.

"I'm going back to bed," Matt Jackson said to no one in particular and did just that.

*   *   *

In his room from where he watched Dr. Abner laughed.

*   *   *

The sun moved. The afternoon came and Dr. Abner walked into Charley's Saloon. As the small man dressed all in black wearing the black hat walked to the bar everyone stopped talking and just froze.

Everyone that is except for Roy Norton, who had just ridden into town not a half hour earlier after a very rugged two weeks at a lumber jack camp chopping trees down.

As soon as Roy collected his pay he'd told the foreman to kiss his ass and that he was done with that type of work. Roy was never going to let anyone ever boss him around again. He was getting his supplies and heading for the mountains and to hell with everybody else.

Of course first on the way he was going to stop in at Totem Lake and drink some beers then go to Hillarie's House of Pleasure and ride a few fillies.

Roy was on his third beer when Dr. Abner walked into Charley's Saloon.

For a while Roy played poker at one of the tables where the local guys seemed more interested in whispering back and forth about what Night Knuckles did to Black Jack Lonagan and the weird goings on around town since then than playing cards. He got bored with that and after winning a few hands threw his cards down and quit.

Roy had a buzz and he was getting happy.

"Who in the hell is this ugly little bastard?" Roy asked the bar tender as the man in black walked past him.

The bar tender ignored Roy.

Dr. Abner reached the bar and smartly turned around and scanned the entire large room of drinking men. There were ten men in the place not counting Roy.

"I need a volunteer," Dr. Abner spoke loudly enough so that there was no doubt everyone could hear him. "I need someone to go and fetch the best prize fighter in this here territory. I hear that man is Jake Killrain and that he is staying at his sister's ranch a little way outside of Stillwell. I will be eternally grateful to whoever takes it upon himself to assist me in this matter."

Everyone in the room, except for one guy, looked the other way and pretended that they never heard a word that Dr. Abner said.

Ever since Dr. Abner had arrived in town with his strange way of talking and his strange way of dressing people had shunned him. This pleased Dr. Abner to no end. Now after the Night Knuckles versus Lonagan fight and the weird things going on, people whispered that Dr. Abner was more than just strange.

He was dangerous.

In fact people considered him so dangerous that the whispering they did was only when they were alone and sure no one could hear.

The only person in Charley's Saloon who didn't act as though he never heard Dr. Abner speak was Roy Norton.

He turned to Dr. Abner at the bar and laughed in his face then said, "Looks like you're just shit out-a-luck little feller."

Dr. Abner looked in Roy Norton's eyes.

"Good," Dr. Abner told him. "You'll do."

Roy said, "What do you got..." He never finished the rest of that sentence. Lights seemed to start blinking at the edge of his vision. The lights grew brighter and the room grew darker. Roy's field of vision telescoped down until it seemed as though he was looking through a long tube and the only thing he could see was Dr. Abner's face.

Dr. Abner spoke slowly and clearly, his voice sounded soothing and melodic. Roy could hear nothing else but Dr. Abner. As he listened Roy Norton cared about nothing else in the world.

"You will go to Stillwell," Dr. Abner told him, "And there you will find the best fist fighter in town and bring him to me. I have heard that this fighter's name is Jake Killrain. Do you understand?"

Roy Norton nodded his head and answered as though he was talking in his sleep. "Yes, I understand. Bring the best fist fighter in Stillwell. And what if he won't come with me?"

"Use any means necessary to get him here. Any!" Dr. Abner said. "Now, be on your way."

Roy Norton turned and instantly walked out of Charley's Saloon. He got on his horse and rode out of Totem Lake.

Dr. Abner looked around the bar room. Everyone avoided his eyes. He liked the feeling of dread that he had awakened in these simple country folk.

This is just like in the old days, he thought, and I will have that kind of power again, only this time, all I seek will be mine.

*   *   *

In the eighth century A.D. Dr. Abner was known as "The Mad Arab" Abdul Alhazred. He was the Sultan's personal necromancer and consultant in the dark arts.

Born during the early part of the eighth century Abdul Alhazred accumulated great wealth and power. His standing in Damascus was second only to the Sultan himself and there were those who believed that he controlled the Sultan and all of his great wealth.

Abdul Alhazred had everything that any man could dream of. He owned huge territories of land. He had a sizable personal army. He owned a harem of hundreds of slave girls of every race to satisfy any hunger he might have.

But it was not enough.

Abdul Alhazred wanted the power of the Gods. Dabbling in the dark arts was not enough. Influencing the lives and decisions of the rich and powerful was not enough. He wanted to become a God.

In his quest to gain the power of the Gods Abdul Alhazred traveled the known and unknown world gathering arcane knowledge.

The knowledge he accumulated were spells and enchantments and black magic from all the ancient religions and warped demonic cults. All of these magic incantations he wrote down and preserved in journals.

These journals became known by a single legendary name; The Necronomicon.

During Abdul Alhazred's fiftieth year on the Earth he tracked down a scroll that was so old that its existence was only whispered about in the most degenerate sects of worshipers of black magic.

The scroll was in a sealed crypt beneath the ancient city of Ur. The chant and ceremony if done correctly was supposed to give the supplicant the power to call upon the Elder Gods and have they do his bidding.

With a legion of warrior slaves to guard him, Abdul Alhazred took laborers and dug the crypt out. Storm clouds swirled above the ancient dead buried desert city as the seal to the crypt was breached.

The daytime sky became so thick with lightning infested storm clouds that it was as dark as night although the hour was twelve noon.

Abdul Alhazred went in by himself carrying an oil lamp because he wanted no other eyes than his own to see the scroll that held the most powerful magic the world had ever known.

Lightning crashed to the ground outside and Abdul Alhazred's warrior slaves cringed together because this desert had never seen a lightning storm the like of this one. The slaves knew that unnatural forces were being toyed with on this night. They trembled and knew fear because these forces were something that they knew they were powerless against.

Down, through deep ever descending tunnels Abdul Alhazred went alone with only the light of his single oil lamp. The passage led far underground, perhaps as far as a mile. It went so far down and deep that the necromancer began to doubt that he would ever see the daylight again.

But he kept going ever deeper.

The stone walls grew moist to his touch and when the passageway finally leveled off he began to see strange hieroglyphics carved into the walls of the tunnel.

The language on the walls was crude pictographs that were mixed with the ancient language of Ur. Abdul Alhazred had deciphered the language of Ur from other tablets found among the ruins so he could understand the written words.

But even if he had not known the words the carved pictures told a story that was awful to behold.

He read the story as he traveled the level stone corridor:

*   *   *

Once, in the beginning, the universe was chaos. Then a guiding light had formed the world and all the creatures upon it. The guiding light went away and left the world populated with multitudes of creatures, men being but one of those.

Behind the guiding light there was a dark force of madness and chaos that worked endlessly to deconstruct all that had been made. That force of chaos created beings of darkness that hid just below the surface of the Earth.

Man was building his first civilizations when the guiding light went away and the beings of darkness came up out of their pits beneath the ground and made slaves of all men.

The beings of the darkness ruled over men with an iron fist and their time was a time of great terror.

When the guiding light came back to check on his creation and saw what had been done to his world he had a great battle with the forces of darkness and won in the end and sent them to exile in a realm just outside this reality.

The beings of darkness came to be known in time as just legends. They were called by many names. All were known as The Elder Gods.

Just as The Guiding Light can never be destroyed neither can The Elder Gods. Both are a part of the universe and can never die.

The Elder Gods always watch man and wait for their chance to come back and begin their next reign of terror.

*   *   *

The hieroglyphic pictographs ended as Abdul Alhazred came to a large steel door. There was a massive steel ring set in that door. He grasped the steel ring and pulled.

The door swung toward Abdul Alhazred easily. He stepped inside.

Inside was a large chamber. The ceiling was so high that it was lost in shadows. The floor was of polished obsidian.

Torches burned at the end of poles that jutted up from the polished black marble floor. The flames looked strange and unnatural.

There were two things in the room that met his eyes.

One was a massive stone oval with symbols from a language he could not read carved into it. Behind the stone oval was the statue of a weird degenerate god from an obscene demented cult.

The statue was that of a beautiful woman's bare torso except that she had eight arms and each hand held a long saw-toothed sword.

The head of the statue was hideous to behold. Long snakes stuck out from where the eyes were and the mouth was enormous with gaping wide open jaws with pointed shark-like teeth.

The other sight was a white ivory table that had one large candle on it that illuminated a single scroll that was rolled up and bound and lying in the center of that table.

Abdul Alhazred knew he found what he came for. He rushed to the table.

He untied the scroll and looked at the words that had not been read for millennia.

The first few lines of the scroll described the chanted spell that made up the bulk of the text.

This was the ancient incantation that Abdul Alhazred had searched his entire life for. This was the spell that would call up an Elder God to do his bidding.

The text stated to even gaze at an Elder God was to become immortal. To command an Elder God was to know unlimited power and unending ecstasy.

Abdul Alhazred laughed and the laugh was the laughter of a man gone insane with the hunger for power.

He began chanting the ancient words written in blood on the scroll. *Why wait to go back to the surface world, he thought. All those up there are as worms to me now.*

At first as he chanted, nothing happened.

Then a high pitched whining sound came to his ears. The sound started softly, so low he could barely hear it. Then it built to a screaming cry that threatened to crush his skull with the high pitch of its vibrations.

The high pitch screeched in his head so loudly that he thought his ears must have blood running from them in rivers. But Abdul Alhazred kept on chanting.

The stone oval now flickered into life. The symbols blinked crimson a few times then began glowing with a weird arcane fire. Inside the center of the oval the air shimmered like the water of a dark pool. It quivered and congealed and with a loud pop the inside of the stone oval became an open doorway that showed the yawning vastness of space.

But this was not the universe we see in the night sky. This was a universe of floating multi-tentacled monstrosities. Some were shaggy. Some were scaly. All of the things that floated in that nothingness were hideous to behold.

All of this Abdul Alhazred saw and still he continued chanting.

He would have his God to command no matter what the cost!

A slimy tentacle reached in over the barrier of the stone oval and grasped its sides. The thing was enormous. It hauled itself slipping and sliding through the opening between the worlds and oozed over the gateway to stop in front of the table that Abdul Alhazred stood at.

Now the chant came to an end and he looked at the thing that he had summoned.

The creature, if that's what it was, raised itself up on the ends of hundreds of tentacles and looked down at Abdul Alhazred. It stood perhaps thirty feet tall, so tall that its head was lost in darkness.

The surface of its shimmering body was dotted with thousands of eyes and hundreds of mouths opened and shut, its lips making smacking sounds. The teeth within every mouth were jagged and gleaming.

"I have summoned you O' Thing from Beyond," Abdul Alhazred shouted at the oozing slime creature before him. "You are here to serve me now."

All of the mouths opened. From the hundreds of hungry throats came the crazed gibbering laughter of insanity.

"We serve no one!" It shouted. "You freed us. We will feed upon you first."

A tentacle snaked out and slapped Abdul Alhazred and knocked him sprawling half unconscious.

The thing came for him.

That was when he saw a golden light, a ball of incredibly warm bright glow appeared in front of the hellish beast from beyond.

The light forced the thing back.

The oozing beast screamed and cursed and swung at the light with its tentacles. The tentacles turned to flame and burned to a crisp as they struck the ball of light.

The Light forced the Thing backward and into the stone oval. Then the stone oval exploded and all went dark.

*   *   *

When Abdul Alhazred awoke he was another man in another body. He was homeless and penniless. He was one of the shunned.

Upon awakening words rang in his ears, *"You who have done the unpardonable will suffer forever upon this Earth. You are cursed to wander forever. You will never know love. You will never know rest."*

Then the voice was gone.

Abdul Alhazred had no name. He used whatever one came to him. He wandered the Earth unwanted and alone.

During the early days of his curse his mind was in a fog. Of those times he remembered little, just endless roaming. All that remained of his former self was his limitless hunger for power.

Gradually, through the centuries, he began to rebuild his abilities to practice magic. With the slow regaining of his psychic strength he learned the power of mesmerism. He could reach out and control the thoughts of others.

He learned other things also.

New sciences of the occult sprang up during the middle ages. One of these new sciences taught him how to animate the dead and make them into hungry engines of destruction that would do his bidding. Through an arcane ceremony where he sacrificed the blood of innocent victims to Dark Gods he could take the dead and let minor demons inhabit them to wreak havoc on the living.

He also learned to resurrect as nosferatu the long dead. He only did this once. That one time was when he found and resurrected the body and the evil spirit of the Viking warrior Ragnar.

By capturing the dead spirit of Ragnar he created a totally obedient servant. By melding that spirit with its resurrected body he created an unbeatable fighting machine.

He now went by the name Dr. Abner and with this warrior he was going to draw crowds that he would lose his resurrected dead upon.

By the time that Dr. Abner was done he would have the largest army the world had ever seen and all of them would obey him without question.

CHAPTER TWELVE
Stillwell

The crowd that initially booed Morrison carried him through the streets and cheered him as a conquering hero. In the lightly falling rain Morrison's name was chanted and songs were sung about his incredible victory over Jake Killrain.

It made him feel good to finally have people on his side but all the well-wishers in the world couldn't fool him to the way these people really were.

Today he'd won. So they all slapped him on the back and called him names like Bombs Away Buckley or Morrison the Mighty.

If he lost tomorrow they'd spit on him and call him a low down scurvy dog.

That was the way of the world. It had always been that way and always would be.

As soon as he got the crowd to let him down Morrison collected his winnings from Barnum. What he was paid was one hundred dollars. It wasn't a fortune but in that day, that was a good chunk of change and would go a long way.

As he was handing over the money Patrick Barnum told Morrison, "You have real talent in those two fists of yours. You could go far but what you need is management."

"Ain't never had a manager," Morrison told Barnum. "Ain't never needed one."

"Which is exactly why you've gotten only as far as you have," Barnum said. "Son, if I can do one thing, it's that I can talk and get things arranged. Stay at my hotel for free for a while and consider having me manage your career. With you having me handle you, I do think that becoming the world champion is only a matter of time."

"I will consider it," Morrison told him and they shook hands. "And I'll need a room for my partner too." He indicated Shingi standing beside him.

"Consider it done," Barnum said and they strode to his hotel where he told the desk clerk to give Morrison and Shingi anything they wanted free of charge.

*　　*　　*

The rooms that Morrison and Shingi were given were side by side and as they were each unlocking the doors to go in Morrison turned to Shingi and said, "I hope you didn't think that it was rude that I didn't have you share my room. You see, now that I'm going to be fighting real professional prize fighters I need to act like a professional myself. The truth is women weaken a man's legs."

Shingi cocked her head considered this and answered.

"It is good that you did not ask me to share your room. I would hate to have hurt your feelings by refusing. You see the real truth is that men weaken a woman's mind."

Morrison unlocked his room and as he entered Shingi surprised him by slipping in past him. She stood in front of him and looked into his eyes.

Morrison smiled at her. She matched his smile. "I thought I just told you," Morrison said, "That I wasn't sharing this room with you because women weaken a fighter's legs."

"You did," Shingi answered him. She came to him wrapping her arms around him and drawing his face down to meet hers. After a long breathless kiss she whispered to him, "If I were an ordinary woman you would be right. But my kind knows things about a man that ordinary women do not even dream of."

Then she spent the night proving to Morrison that what she had told him was not just empty words.

As the night passed away and the dim light of dawn grayed the horizon Morrison saw that Shingi was dressing and getting ready to leave.

"Where are you going?" He asked her. "I thought we did alright last night. Was anything wrong?"

"Everything was perfect, "Shingi told Morrison. "But until my task is accomplished I must not give my life to a man. For now, that is the way that it must be."

Then she went back to her own room.

When Morrison got up later he did have to admit that he felt lighter in his step and generally just stronger. *Yes, that Indian woman did know things, he thought. He'd have to find out more of what she knew in the future.*

*   *   *

Taking full advantage of the offer that Barnum made them both Morrison and Shingi had wash tubs brought to their rooms and filled with hot water. The baths made the both of them feel like new people.

After an hour of lounging around on the big soft bed in his hotel room Morrison went and knocked on Shingi's door. She answered and he asked her to join him for dinner in the hotel's dining room.

The two ordered steak dinners and while waiting for the food to come Shingi told Morrison, "I do not deserve what you are sharing with me. I did no fighting and have nothing to pay for what you give me."

Morrison told her, "If it wasn't for you I probably wouldn't have won that fight. So you don't owe me anything."

Shingi looked perplexed.

"I hadn't had a good meal for months," He told her. "That squirrel and rabbit and those other plants you found for us to eat is what carried me through when the fight got long and hard. You earned everything you're getting."

The steaks came and they smelled delicious.

They dug in.

Shingi ate slowly and savored every bite. She knew that what lay ahead of them would test every bit of strength that they both had.

CHAPTER THIRTEEN
On The Road to Stillwell

Roy Norton rode his horse down the trail under a darkening overcast sky. He didn't exactly know why he was going to Stillwell to fetch the best fighter in the territory. He just knew that he had to.

Roy had been on his horse for six hours straight without a let up. He was tired and needed rest. Stillwell was around a hundred miles south of Totem Lake so the journey there was going to take at least a week.

For the tenth time that day he asked himself, *What the hell am I doing this for? I don't want to go to Stillwell.*

Instantly the inside of his skull erupted in pain. It felt like a red hot needle was being dragged back and forth behind his forehead just above his eyes.

He forced any thoughts of not going from his mind and kept on riding. Roy was getting faster at forcing his own thoughts to go away. The pain that lanced through his head was teaching him how to do what he was instructed to do without Roy thinking about what he wanted.

Pain was an extremely good teacher.

Roy kept riding and the sky kept getting darker until finally the clouds burst open and rain showered down.

When he came to a place where there was a covering of trees Roy found a dry spot and stopped for the night. There he built a fire and ate some jerked beef he had in his saddle bags and lay down to sleep upon the hard ground.

Roy decided right then that in the morning he would start out again. He would go to Stillwell, get directions to where Jake Killrain was and bring him back to Totem Lake.

He would do it without questioning or thinking at all about what he wanted. After that, Roy would put as much distance between himself and everybody else as he could.

Roy was the kind of man who never really liked people anyway. He could take them or leave them. But now that he'd found out there were actually people walking around like Dr. Abner that could reach right into your head and squeeze your brain and make you do things that you didn't want to do, all he wanted to do was leave them.

Roy didn't want to have nothing to do with anybody anymore. These thoughts did not cause him any pain. He guessed that as long as what he thought had nothing to do with disobeying Dr. Abner then he could think about anything he wanted to.

He rolled on his side and tried to drift off to sleep thinking about the girls at Hillarie's House of Pleasure. Roy closed his eyes and pictured ripe breasts, soft lips and creamy thighs. Thoughts didn't give him any pain, no pain at all.

CHAPTER FOURTEEN
Stillwell

With the rising of the sun came a knock on Morrison's door.

Buck threw on his pants and shielded his eyes from the morning sun blasting in through the window and walked to the door. He moved slowly and kind of stiff.

Buck hadn't notice it much the day before but that fight with Killrain had him sore as hell now. It usually did take a few days for the bruises to settle in before the healing actually started. This morning, Buck's bruises were talking to him.

He'd have to see if pretty soon he could get another of Shingi's treatments. That woman sure could take the hurt away.

He opened the door.

Patrick Barnum was there.

"Top of the morning to you," Barnum said in his usual jovial voice. It sounded like a shout this morning.

"What the hell is wrong with you?" Morrison asked. "First time I've been in a comfortable bed in a long while and you come and roust me out of it."

"I've got to get your answer to my question," Barnum said. "The world waits for no man. The early bird gets the worm and..."

"I ain't no dam bird," Morrison told him. "I'll see you in two hours!" He slammed the door in Barnum's face.

* * *

Two hours later Morrison walked into the hotel's dining room and went to the table where Shingi sat with Barnum.

Shingi was wearing a pair of blue jeans and a plaid shirt.

"Where'd you get the new duds?" Morrison asked.

Barnum answered, "I noticed the young lady only had one set of clothes with her so I had her go with one of the girls from my kitchen to The General Store and pick out whatever she liked."

"These are easy to move in," Shingi said. "They're comfortable to wear. I like them."

"Glad you're happy," Morrison told her.

Barnum said, "Now, about what I was going to ask you."

Morrison cut him off. "I'll take you on as my manager," he said. "But I decide who and when I fight. Is that clear?"

"Of course," Barnum answered. "As long as one of the men we fight is Sullivan."

"That's what I'm in this for," Morrison told him and they sealed the deal with a hand shake.

*   *   *

That day was spent setting up a training facility.

There was an empty shed behind Barnum's stable that was used mainly for storing old saddles and stuff like that. Now it was empty except for some trash.

Barnum had a few of his hotel maids clean it out. Then he went with Morrison and Shingi over to The General Store and told the clerk there to give Morrison anything he wanted and put it on his account.

The first thing Morrison picked out was some shoes with rubber soles. The kind of foot gear he had on were cowboy boots.

They were great for riding a horse or doing other cowboy stuff, but for fist fighting they were terrible. The hard soles slid in the dirt too easily for you ever to get a proper grip on the ground to deliver fast hard punches. With the new shoes that wouldn't be a problem anymore.

Thinking about how well he would be able to move and punch with rubber beneath his feet Morrison figured he probably would hand out such a beating to his next opponent that he might start to feel real sorry for the for the guy as he knocked the hell out of him. He told himself right then that he'd have to resist that impulse.

Morrison next picked out a big fifty pound heavy duty burlap bag of dry navy beans with a rope drawstring at the top. Then he picked out a huge roll of masking tape.

"I'll hang the bag up and wail the daylights out of it," He told the clerk. "Wrapping the bag in tape will keep me from punching holes in it."

The clerk looked unimpressed.

"And what the hell," Morrison told him, "If I get my ass kicked I can at least cook up the beans and have something to eat for a few days."

The clerk didn't even smile.

Morrison went around the store and picked out some loose clothing to do his workouts and running in. The last thing he picked out were several rolls of medical gauze wraps. He didn't want to break his hands while in training before he even got to the fight.

All this stuff he hauled over to the shed behind Barnum's stable.

Shingi helped him carry the stuff over and Barnum went off to attend to his own business dealings.

When they got to the shed two men were waiting for them. Both of the guys were young cowboy types who didn't look like they had half a brain between the two of them.

One of them opened the door to the shed as Morrison and Shingi approached.

"What are you guys doing here?" Morrison asked them.

The larger one, a dull eyed guy whose nose looked like it had been on the wrong end of a mule's kick answered. "Barnum sent for us to help you train."

The other one who smiled broadly and showed the world that all his lower teeth were missing and that the top ones were dark brown said, "We're a supposed to be your sparring partners and do whatever the hell you tell us to do."

Morrison thought, *Jesus save us from the idiots!*

He said, "As long as Barnum's paying I don't care who he gets."

71

He told them to hang the bag. When that was done Morrison told them they could leave.

"But Mr. Barnum told us we were supposed to be slinging fists with you today," The guy with no lower teeth said.

"Don't be so anxious for me to raise knots on your head," Morrison told him. "There'll be enough time for that tomorrow. I'll let Barnum know that you did a little work. Be back here at sun up. We start training then."

The two guys wandered off down the street looking sad because some-one hadn't hit them in the face yet.

Morrison turned to Shingi as they watched the boys walk off.

He said, "Guys like that is the reason why the first thing I learned how to do was get out of the way of a punch. You get hit too much, that's what happens to you."

CHAPTER FIFTEEN
Totem Lake

Where the hell are all the people? Sheriff Matt Jackson asked himself as he looked out the door of the Jail House and saw only bare streets. Except for a few horses tied up out in front of Charley's Saloon and some piano music drifting over from Hillarie's House of Pleasure, Totem Lake could have been a ghost town.

If you looked closely you could see that the majority of the shops had open signs in their windows and the shop keeps were inside but there was nobody on the streets. What it got down to was if a person didn't have to be in town they were staying away.

And all this had happened in just a few days, the Sheriff thought.

What I aught to do, the Sheriff said to himself, *is go around and ask people about the Millers to see if there was anyone who might have had a grudge against them.* A lancing, blinding pain shot through Matt Jackson's head.

He staggered backward inside and closed the door. Matt Jackson went and sat in his chair behind his desk and waited for the headache that he'd been battling for the last few days to subside. The Sheriff couldn't remember exactly when the headache started, but it was a doozy.

When the pain started, all that he could do was stop what he was doing and sit down and close his eyes for a few minutes and wait for it to go away.

Eventually, it did.

Yesterday had been a nightmare.

It didn't help that first he'd woke up with a hangover with the owner of Wesley's Gun Smith Shop pounding on his door for him to go see about a burglary where nothing was taken.

When he got done there, Matt came back to the Jail House to catch some more sleep and no sooner had he closed his eyes than someone else was beating on his door.

The Undertaker, Clive Oubben was the one doing the knocking. Clive was a tall skinny man with pasty white skin and real long arms and legs. He always wore a black stove pipe hat and only black clothes. He reminded the Sheriff of a big sickly spider.

Something about the Undertaker made Matt Jackson feel uncomfortable. He wasn't quite sure what. Maybe it was just the idea of a man touching all those dead bodies on a daily basis as part of his job. The Sheriff couldn't understand how anyone could get used to something like that.

The Undertaker stuck his hand out to the Sheriff to shake. He was one of those guys who did that kind of thing and it always gave the Sheriff a case of the goose bumps to even think about touching Oubben's hand. With only the slightest hesitation the Sheriff shook the Undertaker's hand.

"I have a serious problem," Clive stated.

"Doesn't everybody?" Matt answered.

"The Millers are gone," The Undertaker said.

This one took a moment to digest.

"Yeah, I know…" The Sheriff started to say only to have Oubben interrupt him.

"Their bodies have vanished," He said.

The Sheriff went behind his desk and sat down and shook his head.

The Undertaker came farther into the Sheriff's office and stood in front of his desk.

How the hell do I handle this one? The Sheriff thought to himself.

"Well, when was the last time you saw them?" He asked Oubben, not quite sure why he was asking it because it didn't mean a dam thing to him whatever the answer was. The Sheriff knew Undertakers don't just misplace corpses.

Clive Oubben had been the Undertaker in Totem Lake for a long time and this had never happened before. At least as far as he knew it had never happened.

The thought flitted through the Sheriff's mind that maybe Clive had taken a liking to touching dead bodies just a little too much and did something he shouldn't have done. He batted that one out of his head as quickly as he could.

Things were bad enough as it was without considering the possibility that the Undertaker had started having himself a cold one every now and then.

Clive spoke. "We put them on the tables when we brought them in yesterday. I got them ready for the embalming, which I always do on the second day. I had already removed Mr. Miller's organs..."

This was something the Sheriff did not want to hear because he just did not want to have that picture in his head, so he waved his hand for the Undertaker to get on with it.

"I locked up the shop as usual around five in the afternoon and they were still there. This morning, I opened up and the Millers are gone," Oubben said.

The next hour was spent looking around the morgue with the Undertaker for places that the bodies could have been stored by accident and questioning the two hired helpers that he had.

The workers didn't know anything and of course the bodies hadn't just been shoved in a closet by mistake. The Sheriff knew doing these things were ignorant but it was his job so he did them just the same.

After they thoroughly searched the morgue Sheriff Matt Jackson went back to the Jail House with the Undertaker following close behind him saying over and over again, "I don't know what I'm going to do. The funeral's in a week and I ain't got no bodies to display for the relatives. I just don't know what to do."

Once they were at the Jail House the Sheriff closed the door behind the two of them and told Oubben to sit down and shut up.

He did as he was told.

"If you have a brain in your head this is what you'll do," Sheriff Matt Jackson told Oubben. "You keep looking for those bodies anywhere it even vaguely occurs to you that they might be, right up until the night before the funeral. If you find them, do what you do to them as quickly as you can. If you don't find them, load a bunch of rocks in them caskets and have a closed casket funeral. If anybody asks you, tell them that they were too disfigured by the murderer to be made to look right and I'll back you up on it.

"If the bodies turn up later, we'll worry about that when it happens."

Clive thought for a moment. Then it was like a light actually went on in the dim recesses of his mind.

He asked, "Do you think we can actually get away with something like that?"

The Sheriff answered, "Why not? If you and your workers can keep your mouths shut, there ain't no reason why anybody needs to know what's in them boxes. The way I see it, those folks were as dead as rocks when they got to your place anyway, so it doesn't do them any harm if you bury them or not."

"I'm glad you feel that way," The Undertaker said.

"One other thing," The Sheriff told him. "Give their families a real bargain on this funeral. You can tell them you had a personal fondness for the Millers and that's why you're charging then that low a price. We both know the real reason why."

"I will do that," Clive Oubben said.

That was yesterday.

Today, the streets were empty.

At least The Sheriff's headache was mostly gone now so he went back to the door and opened it again.

Dark rain clouds were starting to roll in and at least there was something happening on the street. About a block up a covered wagon that looked packed to the gills was rolling in the direction of the Jail House.

As it got closer and the Sheriff kept watching he saw that it was Ralph Butler, his wife Maureen, and their son Jimmy.

Ralph drove straight on down the street, straight to the Jail House and stopped right out front. He climbed down from the wagon, helped his wife down while the boy jumped to the ground from the other side.

They walked up the steps to the Jail House and this time it was Matt who stuck his hand out first for a shake. Ralph Butler was the town blacksmith and a good checkers player to boot. Ralph had stopped by many times to while away the hours when business was slow for the two of them and Matt always enjoyed his company.

They shook hands and Matt asked, "Where are you all heading to? Rain's coming in. That may not make for easy traveling."

"We're heading out to anywhere but here," Ralph said. "Look around you. Something's got a hold on this town. We're getting out while we can. Whatever's happening here I don't want it to happen to my wife and boy."

The empty streets looked threatening right then, like there was a disease that was ridding Totem Lake of all life.

"I understand what you mean." The Sheriff told them. "And I do wish you well."

"You could come with us," Ralph said. "We sure could use the company on the trail."

Matt considered that.

He breathed heavy, then sighed and answered, "I took an oath to protect this town and I gotta try to do that."

"I reckon so," Ralph told him. We're heading east. If you change your mind, look for us that way."

Matt shook little Jimmy's hand to show him the respect for the man he would become some day and gave Maureen a hug and shook Ralph's hand once again. The family climbed back aboard their wagon.

Ralph flicked the reins and the horses started pulling the wagon again.

He threw back over his shoulder, "Matt, don't wait until it's too late to go. Pretty soon you may not have a town here for you to protect."

Sheriff Matt Jackson looked up and down the empty streets one more time. He knew exactly what Ralph was talking about.

CHAPTER SIXTEEN
Stillwell

When Buckley Morrison showed up at his training shed at sun-up the two guys who wanted him to punch them in the face were already there and waiting for him. It turned out that the two of them were brothers. Their names were Clyde and Curt Hanson.

They lived in town because their father had had enough of them breaking things out on his farm. He couldn't afford to have them around because whenever they tried to do any work for him whatever equipment they used, they broke.

In town they did whatever odd jobs they could get paid for. At least their breaking ways hadn't followed them into town. It must have been because they were a little more careful than when they were working for their Daddy.

The Hanson boys were as dumb as bricks but if you were willing to pay them, they were reliable.

Morrison told Clyde and Curt that the first thing he wanted to do each morning was to go for a good long run.

The Hanson's said they'd be happy to go with him so they set out on the edge of town running around the outside of the buildings that bordered Stillwell.

The morning was cool and overcast but it wasn't raining. It was good running weather. The ground was damp from yesterday's shower but it was not muddy.

After two times around the outside of Stillwell Morrison estimated that he'd ran about five miles and headed back to the training shed.

The Hanson Brothers were already back there. Both of them had given up the run after the first time around. When Morrison showed up they were both sitting back against the wall looking half dead.

"You'll have to get used to this kind of thing," Morrison told them. "Sometimes the sparring is harder than the fights. You've got to be in shape to be able to take what's dished out during practice."

"Are you going to dish us up some of them knuckle sandwiches today?" Clyde asked. He was the larger one, the one with good teeth.

"Yeah, we'll give that a little bit of a shot later," Morrison said.

Morrison told The Hanson Brothers to wrap the hanging fifty pound bag of beans with the masking tape.

While they did that he wrapped his hands. He never let anyone else do that. Hands wrapped the right way fused the bones together and prevented your hand from being broken when you landed a good punch. Hands wrapped the wrong way were worse than no wraps at all. They'd cause the bones to separate when a punch landed causing breaks and ligament tears.

When the bag was taped and his hands were wrapped, Morrison had Curt Hanson time him on the bag. He pounded the bag steadily with every punch in his arsenal for three, ten minute time periods.

By the time he was done with that Morrison was covered with a coating of sweat and his arms were beginning to feel heavy and tired.

Now was the perfect time for him to do a little bit of sparring. No one needs to know how they throw punches when they are fresh. Everybody who knows how does it the right way before they get tired. The time to spar is when you're fatigued so that your mistakes are amplified and you can be aware of them and not make that mistake in a real fight.

Morrison chose Curt to spar with first. He was smaller, so Morrison figured he should be faster than his brother.

Before they started Morrison told the two of them, "Remember, we're here to train. We're not here to try to knock the crap out of each other."

"OK," Curt said to Morrison. "I'll try not to hurt you."

"I appreciate that," Morrison told him.

Morrison had Clyde time them. They were set to do one, ten minute round. When they were both ready, Morrison told Clyde to start the clock.

Then he said, "Let's go!"

Curt surprised him by not rushing in. He made all kinds of weird faces and flapped his hands out in the air all around his head while moving in a circle in a kind of strange dance.

Morrison knew that this guy had never even seen a prize fight but at least he was using a little bit of imagination to try to figure out what he was supposed to do.

Morrison feinted at Curt's head so he'd throw both hands up, then he rushed in and grabbed him in a bear hug.

While he had him in a tight grip Morrison told him, "Good job on using your head, but you don't have to move around this much to have a good defense. If you move as much as you have been, you'll be tired in no time. We'll go light and I'll give you pointers as we go."

Then he let Curt loose.

Curt quit moving but he still was waving his hands in the air like someone trying to catch moths.

"I'll show you why you shouldn't move your hands all the time," Morrison told him.

He faked a right to Curt's stomach and both of Curt's hands dropped. When they did, Morrison threw an open handed slap to Curt's jaw to let him know his mistake.

Morrison stopped in the middle of the ring and said, "Keep your hands open and up." He demonstrated by putting his hands in the proper place. "Just like this. And keep your elbows in to your sides too. That helps block body punches. If you get hit on your side real hard without blocking some of the force, the next day you'll be pissing blood and believe you me, that don't feel too good."

Curt did what Morrison told him and became a harder target almost immediately.

Morrison didn't throw any punches to hurt Curt. He just tapped him every now and then to show him where the hole in his defense was.

He also had to show Curt the proper way to throw a punch. Every time Curt attempted a punch he drew his arm back and wind milled his fist out wide of the mark.

The ten minute round was more like a boxing lesson than sparring but at least Morrison did get some exercise and Curt did seem to be picking up what he was told.

When they were done he told Morrison, "That was fun. I think I done learned enough so that in a few weeks I'll be beating the tar out of you."

Morrison laughed and answered, "In a few weeks when you do get better at boxing you won't think this is so much fun. Right now, for me to get anything out of sparring with you, I got to teach you how to spar."

Then it was Clyde's turn.

When Curt was ready to start the timing and Morrison said go, Clyde charged him with his head down like an enraged bull.

Morrison stepped to the side and tied him up and told him, "This is training Clyde. You need to take it easy."

"Take it easy hell!" Clyde yelled. "Now you're tangling with the big brother. I'm gonna have to show you how it's done boy."

Morrison knew there wasn't going to be any reasoning with this guy so he let him go and stepped away from him saying, "You come at me like that again and I'll show you why I do this for a living."

Clyde spit into his hand and rubbed them together then slicked his hair back with it. He put his head down and charged again swinging haymakers as he came.

Morrison stepped to the side and slipped in a short right uppercut to Clyde's nose.

Clyde straightened up holding his nose with his left hand and said, "Hey, you..."

That was all he got out because Morrison put him on his back with a hard left hook.

Curt went to his dazed brother on the ground and helped him to a sitting position.

"When I tell you to take it easy, I mean it!" Morrison told the two of them.

The rest of that day Morrison spent trying to explain and demonstrate the basics of what made up a skilled bare-knuckle boxer. To their credit the

Hanson Brothers did try to listen and do what they were told. But Morrison knew it was going to be a long hard road ahead before either one of them would be a good training partner.

One side effect from that first day of sparring was that once Clyde got over the embarrassment of being knocked on his ass, he started following Morrison around like his new puppy. After their day of training would be over, him and Curt would ask Morrison what he was going to be doing, then they wanted to tag along no matter what it was.

It got so bad that he had to start telling them things like, "Hey boys, I think I'm going to go take me a crap now. When I start squeezing one off, it's a frightening experience to witness. I sure don't need your company for that and it's bad for your health to be inhaling those vapors too. So why don't you go find somewhere else to be."

During the fourth day of training Shingi came out to the shed and was watching what was going on. She seemed bothered by something so when he was done doing his bag work and the hand speed drills that he'd thought up for himself Morrison sent The Hanson's off on some errand and came over to her.

"I need to talk to you," Shingi told him.

"Well, we're partners," Morrison said. "So go ahead and say what's on your mind."

In the short time that Morrison had known Shingi he'd come to under-stand that she was the easiest person to talk to that he'd ever known. They always had breakfast together and usually had dinner together. Being with her was not like it was when he had been with any other woman. If he felt like telling her what happened during his day, he did. If he didn't, then he didn't.

There was no need for either one of them to try to impress the other. Both of them were at ease in the other's presence like they had known each other for many years.

It was because of this innate trust in each other that Shingi spoke to Mor-rison the way she did now.

"There is something evil that we must defeat," she told him. "It calls to us. I can feel it coming closer."

"Well, what is it?" Morrison asked.

Shingi told Morrison of her dream of a white man's town being invaded by the enormous spider who gave birth to hundreds of smaller spiders who devoured the town's inhabitants.

Then she told him of talking with the Great Spirit of the Earth at Morrison's campsite and being told that their destinies were locked together. She also told him the vision she was shown about his early life and his fight with O'Dowd.

This last bit surprised the hell out of Morrison because he'd never told Shingi anything about his childhood and definitely nothing about his short slugfest with Professor Mike O'Dowd.

In fact, he hadn't thought anything at all about O'Dowd for years.

The truth of the matter was, Morrison had wanted to get O'Dowd back in the worst way and when he came of age and left the orphanage it took him five years but he tracked O'Dowd down in Houston Texas.

By then, any thought of revenge was far past due. O'Dowd was an old broken down alcoholic living in a flop house. Beating on him wouldn't have been a contest, just an act of cruelty.

"The reason we've been brought together," Shingi told Morrison, "Is to stop the evil thing that I know is now coming for us."

"How are we supposed to know where this thing is you're talking about?" Morrison asked.

"I do not know." Shingi answered.

"Well, what I got to do is beat the best fighter in the world," Morrison said. "That's what I live for. A man's got to have a goal and that's mine. If that evil thing you're talking about ends up being the best fighter in the world then I guess I'll end up fighting him."

"I understand," Shingi told Morrison. She knew he was the kind of man who made up his own mind and when he did no one could change it for him. "Perhaps the Great Spirit of the Earth was wrong and we should not be together. I only know one thing. I know I will fight this evil thing. If need be, I will fight it alone."

CHAPTER SEVENTEEN
Totem Lake

The sky was slate grey and getting darker. Shadows were growing longer. Evening was coming.

Deputy Don Carson was finishing up his walk around check for the day. The Deputy and the Sheriff these days were trading off on doing the rounds.

For the last three days neither one of them had done rounds after dark. They knew that something was on the streets of Totem Lake at night, something that guns were no protection against.

The Deputy climbed the three stairs to the Jail House and stopped. He leaned his long lean frame against the wall beside the door. Don Carson was taller and slimmer than the Sheriff.

He looked up and down the street. It was eerie.

No one was outside on the street at all. There weren't even any horses out in front of Charley's Saloon.

At this time at the end of the day usually the first lamps of the evening were being lit. On this evening there were no lights coming from inside any windows.

Totem Lake had the look of a town where everyone had just packed up and left. Deputy Don Carson knew that was not really the case, even though he wouldn't have blamed anyone if they did leave.

Earlier while doing his walk around check seeing that most of the houses in town looked deserted from the outside the Deputy had tried some doors. A few of them had been locked but most had been nailed shut from the inside. Wood had also been nailed across the windows of most homes to keep out … God knows what.

All of this was unnerving, so unnerving that the Deputy himself, who used to stay in a complimentary room above Charley's Saloon now slept in one of the Jail House cells.

He locked himself in at night.

The Jail House was now the safest place to be after the sun went down. There were bars on all the windows.

The Deputy went in through the Jail House door. He sat down in a chair in front of the Sheriff's desk.

Sheriff Matt Jackson was playing a game of solitaire. He looked up from his cards.

"Any change?" He asked.

"Not really," Don Carson told him. "Except more people are gone and the ones left are nailing their doors shut and boarding up their windows."

They both sat in silence for a few minutes.

The Deputy watched as the Sheriff finished off a stack.

"What the hell are we still doing here?" Don Carson asked.

The Sheriff looked up from his cards again.

"I took an oath to protect the people of this town," he said. "That's why I'm here. You're welcome to leave any time you feel like it."

Sheriff Matt Jackson slid open the drawer to his desk. He took out a bottle of rot gut whiskey. He took a big drink from the bottle, grimaced and shook real hard till the goose bumps the whiskey gave him went away.

"Let me have a slug of that," the Deputy said and took the bottle from the Sheriff's hand.

He took his drink and his body trembled as badly as the Sheriff's had.

"Lord! That is some horrible tasting shit," he told the Sheriff.

"The worst I could get," Sheriff Matt Jackson told him. "I bought an entire case of it for next to nothing and it's worth exactly what I paid."

They traded drinks for the next half hour until the whiskey was making their faces feel warm and the sun set completely behind the horizon.

"So are you leaving or what?" The Sheriff asked his Deputy.

Don Carson went to the window and slid the shade to the side. Night was in full bloom now. No lights were coming from any windows.

Even the doors to Charley's Saloon were closed and locked. The street was in full twilight.

Down the ways a bit, perhaps a quarter of a block down, three shadows raced from the blackness between two buildings to the darkness between a few other shops.

Other shadows moved in the distance. The shadows were not people. The Deputy knew that. Not any more, anyway.

He closed the curtain and turned back to the Sheriff.

"No, I'm not leaving," Don Carson said. "Not tonight I'm not."

He reached for another drink from the whiskey bottle.

"Besides," he said. "Where could I go and get such great free liquor?"

"Nowhere," Sheriff Matt Jackson told him and they drank until they couldn't drink any more.

CHAPTER EIGHTEEN
Stillwell

Roy Norton was filthy and dog tired when he arrived in Stillwell in the middle of the night. He rode his horse straight to Black Betty's Brew House. In these frontier towns the local saloon was usually the quickest place to get information about what was going on in the area.

In the front, outside of Black Betty's was a watering trough. Roy let his horse go to the trough and drink his fill. He went to it and leaned over and splashed water on his face. Then he stuck his head in.

The cool water felt good after all the hours on horseback he'd spent that day. Five days after leaving Totem Lake Roy Norton was in Stillwell. He had traveled hard and fast. It wasn't riding that would set any world records but this was the fastest journey Roy had ever made.

Every time Roy slowed down and wasn't at the point of exhaustion that damn headache had come on him again like a spike being driven into his brain. The pain drove him on until he just couldn't go any more. Then, he'd stop, eat fast, sleep till he woke up, and then head out fast again.

Now, he was here.

He was going to find out where Jake Killrain was and go get him.

Roy stood up from the trough and let the water run off his head and down into his shirt and onto his chest and back. It wasn't quite as good as a bath but for now it would have to do.

He went in through the bat wings and walked directly to the bar.

Black Betty herself was tending bar. She was a big deep chocolate colored Negro woman who wiggled when she walked and jiggled when she laughed.

Black Betty jiggled a lot.

She went to the stranger at the bar.

"What can I get for you?" She asked with a big toothy smile breaking out of her big round face.

"A beer," Roy Norton said and started digging into his pocket.

A flash of pain shot through Roy's head. He was very familiar with that pain.

"And some information," he added as Black Betty handed him his filled glass and he paid her.

"I need to know where I can find Jake Killrain," Roy said.

"I suppose he's still out at his folks spread licking his wounds," Black Betty told him.

The question flashed through his mind, *What's he licking his wounds from?* But just as the thought came up he pushed it away. Roy was anticipating that next jolt of pain that was going to be lancing through his head.

He knew if he got to talking about anything other than what was going to get him to Killrain the pain would be coming sooner than later.

"Jake's an old friend of mine from back east," Roy said. "I heard he was in the territory and want to go by and pay him a visit."

"It's at least a four hour ride," Black Betty told Roy Norton.

"That's alright with me," Roy answered. "Let me know where he is and I'll just head out in the morning."

Black Betty gave Roy directions to the Killrain spread and Roy downed his beer in one gulp."

"Thank you kindly," Roy told the large black woman and turned and started walking toward the door.

"You mean you ain't gonna have another one darlin'," Black Betty asked in a mock hurt tone. "I thought you just said you were waiting till morning to go out there. Why I could get the notion that my company ain't wanted."

She winked at Roy and her smile was an open invitation.

Roy smiled himself and threw back over his shoulder, "It just occurred to me that my business with Jake just can't wait. When I can I'll come back and see you."

Then he was out the door.

At the water trough Roy blew a sigh of relief. Close call, he thought. *Having a go with that woman would be like wrestling a grizzly bear, interesting, but it was bound to be a bruiser.*

Roy mounted his horse and rode out of town toward the Killrain place.

Two hours later he was dead in the saddle so he stopped under a big pine tree, built a small fire and rested until dawn.

*　　*　　*

Dawn came *far* too early.

When Roy woke up the first thing he did was turn over away from the sun to try and go back to sleep.

The pain in his head came again telling him to get up.

He stood and shook his head to clear some the morning cobwebs out and mounted his horse and rode on.

*　　*　　*

The Killrain Place was a rather large spread of land.

They had a ten acre apple orchard, a few acres of wheat fields and somewhere around twenty acres of open grazing land where a small herd of cows wandered around chewing grass with dull sleepy eyes until the bulls would have a go at them. That always woke the cows up for at least a few minutes.

Roy Norton rode past all that and headed for the main house, a three story six bedroom home that was trying hard to look like a well-to-do pre-Civil War Mansion in the Old South. He rode up to the house, tied his horse on the hitching post and used the knocker.

After rapping about ten times the door was answered by a slightly built cute nineteen year old girl with freckles, blond hair in pig tails, and green eyes.

She smiled and said, "Howdy Mister. Wha...," and her ill-fitting dentures clacked together and pretty much jumped out of her mouth and flew at Roy.

Norton back peddled away from the attacking teeth and they bounced down the two front steps and took a snap at the ground burying the biting surface a half inch in the dirt.

"Oh...thyit!" The girl shouted chasing her teeth down and stomping on them with one of her bare feet to make sure they didn't get away.

"Da dam dangs won't tay on my muckin' mout!" She yelled to no one in particular.

A man's voice came booming from behind her in the house. "You quit that dam cussin' Clara!"

"Muck quew!" She yelled at the voice from inside. Clara grabbed her teeth from out of the dirt. She held them up in front of her face inspecting them with one squinting eye.

They must have passed inspection because she blew on them and dirt flew from between some of the teeth, then she slipped them back in her mouth and stormed inside leaving Roy Norton standing at the foot of the two stairs.

From inside Roy heard, "Don't you come sassing at me woman. Them's the best dam teeth I could get on short notice. Now go wash your mouth out. You got mud dripping off those things."

A well-muscled man with a handlebar mustache and a bandaged nose appeared at the front door.

"I need to speak to Jake Killrain," Roy Norton told him.

"You're already doing that," the man told him. "So what do you need?"

Roy could see the wounds that Black Betty had referred to. Both of Jake Killrain's eyes had dark yellowish purple bruising and there were several abrasions around his cheeks from knuckles. He also had a good sized knot in the middle of his forehead that almost looked like he was getting ready to grow a third eye.

Jake saw Roy studying his battle marks and quickly said, "Don't worry about those, they're nothing. I've had worse on my tongue and chewed cornbread. What are you here for?"

"I was sent here to bring you back to Totem Lake for a fight," Roy said.

Jake Killrain laughed. "I won't be fighting anybody for a long while. This here is a broken nose," he said and pointed at his bandaged snoz. "Until this is completely healed, I ain't fighting anyone. And when this here nose is healed I'm gonna have me another go at the man that broke it for me.

"I'll know what to expect next time and I'll beat him like a rug hung out with the wash."

Roy asked, "So you fought someone just recently and he beat you?"

"Only because of a surprise attack," Killrain snarled the blood rising to his face.

"Hold on there Jake," Roy quickly said. "I ain't meaning to rile you up. I was just sent out here to find the best fighter around Stillwell and I thought that was you."

"I still am the best fighter in this here territory," Killrain snapped. "It's just that temporarily he's got this fake little title they made up, Champion of Stillwell, that they gave him after he fought me. When I'm prepared I'll beat him eight days a week and don't you forget that!"

"Well, I should be on my way," Roy told Killrain. "I got a long ride ahead of me. With that broken nose of yours I'm going to have to get this other guy."

"Hold on a moment," Killrain said. "Who's this guy you're setting up the fight for anyway?"

"I was sent out here by the man who handles a fighter called Night Knuckles. He's the meanest son of a bitch you'd ever dream of seeing."

Roy then told Jake Killrain the story of the fight between Night Knuckles and Black Jack Lonagan that he'd heard from the guys he played cards with at Charley's Saloon.

When he finished Killrain said, "Lord! This Night Knuckles sounds like a monster."

"He is," Roy Norton told him.

Killrain thought for a moment then said, "Come on in for a moment. I got to tell the old battle ax I'm taking off. If this Night Knuckles is as bad as you say he is and you do sound like you believe what you say, then I don't want no part of him. I'm a bad man but I ain't stupid. I'm also gonna make

92

sure he does get his hands on this Buck L. Morrison. The easiest way for me to be rid of him, would be to feed him to Night Knuckles.

"I learned a long while back, around the same time that I fought John L. Sullivan that no matter how good you are there's always somebody out there who can beat you and sometimes it's better to let somebody else do the dirty work."

Killrain took Norton into the house and told him to sit in a chair. Everything in the house was piled up with soiled clothes, beer bottles and just about any kind of trash you could name. Roy could see that even with all the money and the land that the Killrain clan had they still lived like filthy degenerate hillbillies.

This, come to think of it, made Roy feel right at home because that's exactly what he was. Roy picked up a pile of trash off one of the chairs and dropped it to the floor then sat down.

Killrain yelled for his misses to bring Roy a glass of cool tea.

Clara appeared a few minutes later with two glasses of tea. She smiled a closed mouth smile and handed Jake Killrain his glass then gave Roy his.

Roy took a large drink. It tasted very cool and sweet going down.

Jake Killrain said to Clara, "I'm leaving. I'm not sure when I'll be back. You'd best be here when I do get back if you know what's good for you."

"Why Jake, why you got to go off and just leave me here?" Clara squawked. With the last word her teeth clacked together again but this time she was able to clamp her chops shut and clap her hand to her mouth and shove her teeth back in before they went flying.

"Because I said I'm going to god-dam-it!" Jake yelled. "I didn't bring you out here to tell me what the hell to do."

Clara took her teeth out and held them in her left hand to talk.

She went on. "You know I'm boy'd twyin' to tock to you dumb fokes. Wha am I sposed to do?"

"Don't talk about my folks like that," He told her. "Ain't nobody dumber than you around here."

Clara started to say something and Jake shouted, "Dam-it woman, just shut up! I get tired of this yappin' all the time."

He pointed at Roy. "Drink that down," He ordered. "We're leaving."

Roy drank his tea down in one gulp.

Jake did the same.

Jake grabbed Roy's glass and shoved the two of them at Clara. "Take these," he said. "I'll see ya, when I see ya."

Clara's eyes looked they were getting ready to tear up. She looked suddenly very sad like she might cry.

"I don't think you love me," Clara whined.

"Course I love ya', dam-it!" Jake told her and leaned forehead and kissed her on the forehead. He spun her around and smacked her on the behind.

"I gotta go do a man's work." He gave her a little shove toward the kitchen.

"Come on," Jake told Roy and they headed out the front door.

Jake Killrain went and got his horse, a black roan, his gun belt and six-shooter, a rifle that he stuck in a scabbard hanging from the side of his saddle, and an ax handle that he stuck into a second scabbard.

Then they rode out toward Stillwell.

CHAPTER NINETEEN
Stillwell

Buck L. Morrison finished off his day of training feeling good. He was over his soreness from the Killrain fight, his wind was fine and he had never felt faster when throwing combinations.

The way he felt right then if the Devil himself jumped up out of his dark pit he'd kick his ass and send him with his tail between his legs limping back to hell.

Morrison never in his life had what could have been called a training camp. Maybe this one wasn't top of the line but he was enjoying the hell out of getting in good shape. He was feeling stronger and faster than he ever felt before. This taking on Barnum as his manager had been a very good idea.

The one person he wanted to tell how good his training was coming along was Shingi. So after storing some of his training gear in the back of his covered wagon Morrison told the Hanson Brothers they could quit for the day. He was intending on taking a bath, finding Shingi and taking her to dinner.

When he dismissed the Hanson Brothers Clyde looked disappointed and said, "Mr. Morrison I've been waiting all day after you was done doing what you planned on doing to get yourself shaped up to ask you if you'd show us some of your special moves so we can give you a harder time sparrin'. I think it'd be better for you if we can feed you back some of those knuckle sandwiches every now and then, so you're used to it when a real good fighter does it."

Morrison knew Clyde did have a point but he also knew that the real reason Clyde wanted to continue that days training was because ever since he'd knocked the crap out of that boy, Clyde had developed a type of hero worship for him. Morrison was feeling good but he didn't want to continue training for that day. *Doing too much can be almost as bad for you as not doing enough.*

He was feeling so good that he told Clyde and Carl, "Tomorrow, I'll begin showing you some moves where it just wouldn't be fair for you to ever use them in a street fight because no one would even have a chance of beating you."

Then he told them. "You boys have worked hard. In an hour meet me at the hotel's dining room. I'm taking us all out to dinner. You both deserve it."

The Hanson Brothers were so excited they jumped up and down and hooted and the two of them grabbed Morrison in a bear hug.

After prying loose from them Morrison told them, "Jesus, you boys carry a powerful stink with you. Make sure you wash and clean up before coming over. The way you smell now, you'd make women fall over."

*   *   *

At the hotel Morrison had a hot bath drawn for him. He scrubbed himself clean and put on some of the nice clothes he bought on Barnum's expense account. Then Morrison went next door and knocked at Shingi's room.

Usually at this time of day Shingi could be found there. What she was doing before Morrison would show up, he didn't have any idea. *Probably just Indian stuff,* he told himself the one time he'd thought about it.

Now when Morrison knocked at her door, there was no answer. He knocked some more then remembered that for the last few days she'd started taking walks around the outside of town. When Morrison had decided to change up his training and ran in the afternoon instead of the morning he'd seen her there.

Outside of town, closer to nature Shingi seemed more at home than in the middle of Stillwell. Shingi had started out in her first few days in town taking walks on her own into the shops around Stillwell. But it was obvious to her that the people were only being polite because she was with Buck L. Morrison.

Shingi now wore the white man's clothes, ate his food, and lived under his roof but to the people of Stillwell, she was still just an ignorant red savage. So now, while Shingi was as polite to them as they were to her, she did not seek out the company of the people of Stillwell.

Except when Shingi spent time with Buck L. Morrison and the people who came to see him, she spent her time in her room or walking in the countryside around the town. The creatures and spirits of the natural world had always been company enough for Shingi.

It had always been that way for her and always would be.

*   *   *

Morrison found Shingi sitting on a grassy hillside to the east of town talking with a prairie dog that ran and disappeared into its hole at his approach.

"What were you two talking about?" Morrison asked her as he dismounted Horse.

"Many things," she answered. "But mainly about how the world has changed and about how much harder it is for both of our kinds to survive in this changing world."

"The only thing constant is change," Morrison told Shingi. "The boys are going to have dinner with us tonight and I came out to find you."

Shingi stood up and called out in a sing song voice, "Good-bye my little friend. I will come back and we will talk again."

The prairie dog stuck his head up out of his hole and gave off a chirping noise then disappeared back down his hole.

"That's strange the way you talk to these animals," Morrison said. "That guy seemed like he knew what you said and answered."

Morrison mounted Horse and Shingi climbed up behind him.

"It is not strange to me," Shingi told him. "The animals understand me and I understand them."

*   *   *

Shingi went and cleaned up and they met the Hanson Brothers in the hotel dining room. They sat at a large table that seated six people and just before the waitress came and gave them menus, Patrick Barnum came into the room and headed straight for their table.

"I hope I'm not imposing if I sit with you," Barnum said. "But I noticed I was hungry and since I saw you were here, I figured why not."

"It's your hotel," Morrison told him. "You can sit wherever you want."

"That is true," Barnum said.

"You are always welcome," Shingi told him.

"Thank you very much little lady," Barnum said pulling out a chair. He sat down.

The waitress brought the menus.

"How's your training coming?" Barnum asked while scanning the selections.

He knew full well what was on the menu since there wasn't but three selections to be had: Steak and potatoes, Chicken and potatoes, Salmon and potatoes.

In this part of the country, in a town of this size, three selections on a menu was highly unusual. Usually a café in a small town just made a lot of one item and if you didn't want that, then you'd better think about eating somewhere else.

"Training's going good," Morrison told Barnum. "That's why the boys are here. They worked so hard I decided to treat them to some grub."

Clyde and Carl had been staring down into their menus like they were trying to decipher ancient Egyptian Hieroglyphics which Morrison realized immediately might have been easier for the boys. He saw that neither of them could read and wondered if Shingi could.

"Well let me see," Morrison said speaking slowly. "I see we got us three choices here. I see I'm going to have to choose between steak and potatoes, chicken and potatoes and salmon and potatoes. I think I'll end up taking the steak. I worked hard today and I'm hungry."

Shingi and the boys knew that he'd spoken like that to help them not be embarrassed by not being able to read. When the time came four steak and potatoes were ordered and Barnum ordered chicken.

While they were eating Barnum told Morrison, "I've sent out a newspaper report about your win over Killrain to Seattle and Tacoma and even had one sent down to Portland to see what kind of interest we can scare up. You're a valuable fighter now.

"When offers come in for fights, and they will, we will accept nothing less than two thousand dollars and ten percent of the gate. I get thirty percent up front. That's standard management fee and we accept no offer without a five hundred dollar advance. I don't want to be wasting our time with someone who makes offers without the money to back it up. How does that sound?"

Morrison answered, "It sure beats the five dollar side bets I was making on myself."

Shingi now spoke. "You have said several times that the one person you want to fight the most is John L. Sullivan, why him?"

Morrison opened his mouth and Barnum started speaking. "John L. Sullivan is the World Heavyweight Champion. He is the acknowledged greatest two fisted Bare-Knuckle warrior on the Earth. To fight John L. Sullivan is to place yourself near the pinnacle of the sporting world. If Buck here were to beat John L. Sullivan then he would become a legend among fighting men, not to mention extremely wealthy."

Barnum took a breath after his spiel and before he opened his mouth again to speak Morrison cut him off.

"Don't ever answer for me again," Morrison told Barnum, his voice even and hard as ice. "I always speak for myself, especially when Shingi asks me something."

"Why I didn't think..." Barnum started.

Morrison cut him off again, "That's right. You didn't think. I ain't one of those prize fighters whose brains have been pounded so much that they can't do nothing but throw punches and grunt. You stick to your management things but when someone asks me a question, I give my answers."

He looked at Shingi and she smiled.

"OK," Morrison said. "The reason I want to fight John L. Sullivan so bad is because he's a disgrace to Bare-Knuckle fist fighters everywhere.

"Barnum is right. The Heavyweight Champion is acknowledged as being the strongest and bravest warrior in the world. Young boys look up to him and imitate him. John L. Sullivan is a drunkard and a braggart. He gets into brawls with men who have no chance of ever beating him.

"The man who is the Heavyweight Champion should cast a noble shadow and be worthy of the title that he owns. John L. Sullivan should not be the Heavyweight Champion and if I get the chance to meet him, I'll be happy to take the title and wear it with the dignity that it deserves."

That was when a man who had just entered the dining room and overheard Morrison's speech came to their table.

Roy Norton spoke directly to Morrison when he said, "I come here on behalf of Dr. Abner, manager of the greatest prize fighter this world has ever seen, Night Knuckles. He offers you the chance to prove that you are the best prize fighter in all the land by coming to Totem Lake and fighting Night Knuckles."

Morrison looked over at Barnum and said, "Well, since you got such a need to talk, here's your chance. Now you get the chance to do your management thing."

CHAPTER TWENTY
Stillwell

Patrick Barnum stood up and extended his hand to Roy Norton and they shook. They introduced themselves.

"What kind of money are we talking about?" Barnum asked.

Norton thought for a moment then said, "We'll arrange that when we get to Totem Lake. Y'all will be paid for appearing at the contest but the majority of the money from this fight goes to Dr. Abner and Night Knuckles. It is a privilege for any man to tangle with Night Knuckles, the Greatest Bare-Knuckle Prize Fighter this world has ever seen."

"So what you're saying is you don't have any money to put up-front as an appearance fee," Barnum said.

From the moment that Roy Norton appeared Shingi's eyes locked on him. She regarded him with a combination of hostility and dread.

Norton answered Barnum, "What I'm saying is Dr. Abner is giving Buck L. Morrison the opportunity to prove his worth in combat. We're not going to pay you to give you an opportunity."

Barnum laughed. "Your man, this Night Knuckler or whatever the hell his name is, is the one seeking opportunity. Buck L. Morrison has proven himself as having international level skills by beating Jake Killrain.

"Your man is nothing until he beats Buck L. Morrison. The price you have to pay for him to enter a ring in Totem Lake against your man is two thousand dollars, five hundred dollars to be paid in advance."

Roy Norton opened his mouth to speak and Barnum raised a finger.

"I'm not through yet," He said. "If you don't have that money, then I won't even waste our time with you. Money talks, bullshit walks. If you ain't got the money, it's time for you to walk son."

Roy Norton looked hard at Barnum, his eyes burning out a threat. "This won't be the last time you'll hear from me!" He said and stomped out the door.

Outside the hotel Roy walked down past two buildings then stepped into the darkness of a walkway between two shops.

A man was standing back away from the light in the shadows.

"I take it that it went the way I told you that it would," Jake Killrain told Norton.

"The bastards wanted money up front," Norton said. "They wanted a lot of it."

"Good," Killrain said. "Now we do it my way."

*   *   *

As soon as Roy Norton left the room Shingi turned to Morrison, "That man was sent by the evil one I told you about," she told him.

"Well, we don't have to worry about him now," Morrison said. "Barnum fixed his water wagon but good."

"This Roy Norton, he stinks of the evil thing that I now know is in the Town of Totem Lake. We must go there," Shingi told him.

"Yeah, I did notice that Norton was kind of ripe," Morrison said.

"The boy kind-a, had a green cloud following him around," Barnum told them.

All the guys laughed.

Morrison leaned over to Shingi and said, "When the time is right, we'll go to Totem Lake."

"That time should be now," Shingi told Morrison but he didn't hear her. He was already joking with the guys again.

*   *   *

The food was good and everybody took their time eating. After the meal was consumed everybody had a few drinks.

Morrison set the tone when the drinks were ordered and he had a soda pop. He told everyone that he didn't drink anything with alcohol in it. The

102

one time he'd done that had been a bad experience that he didn't want to repeat.

The Hanson Brothers followed Morrison's example and had soft drinks. Shingi had lemonade. Lemonade was the one thing that Shingi loved about the white man's civilization. As far as she was concerned they could keep everything else but she loved drinking lemonade.

Barnum drank a dark bitter beer and when he was half way through his first stein he told Morrison, "You're the first prize fighter I ever met that wasn't a drinker. Why don't you drink?"

"I have my reasons," Morrison told them all. "And none of them that I'm proud of."

Barnum said, "Come on. We're all here among friends. There's nothing you could say that would change that."

The Hanson Brothers looked eager to hear a story but didn't want to step out and say so.

Shingi simply said, "You do not have to tell anything about yourself that you do not want to."

That was what decided it. For some reason Morrison wanted Shingi to know this story. About the others, well what the hell, they were there and he could care less if they heard this or not."

"The story is simple," Morrison started. "Back when I had just left the orphanage, as a matter of fact, six months after, I found myself in Kansas City Missouri.

"I got myself a job selling newspapers and saved every penny I had till I had myself a little bit of pocket change.

"I was doing all right for myself, had a place I was renting, clothes on my back. I had a few extra pairs of drawers in the closet. I was slowly moving up in the world.

"Then with some money in my pocket I met this cute blond headed woman. I didn't know a thing about women then and when she smiled at me I kind of lost all my marbles over her.

"She wanted me to buy her a drink, so I did. Of course I bought myself a whole lot of them too. Before I knew it, I was looped but good. She wanted to go back to my place so I took her back there.

"Three of her friends followed us back to my place. I was too dammed drunk to fight but I tried anyway and they beat me to within an inch of my life.

"The three guys and the woman stripped my home bare. I woke up with nothing but a bad ass whipping and a seriously bruised ego to show for my good time."

Morrison looked right at Clyde and Carl then.

"Do you know what the moral of this story is?" He asked them.

They both shook their heads no.

He told them. "It should be obvious. Don't drink. It'll make you do stupid things. I ain't drank since that day, ain't ever going to either."

The party broke up after that.

Barnum went to his room in the hotel. Clyde and Carl went to the place that they shared down the street and Morrison and Shingi went to their rooms.

Outside their rooms Shingi turned to Morrison and told him, "We need to go to Totem Lake. It is our destiny to face what is there."

Morrison opened his door a crack then answered her. "Don't worry about it. We'll get to Totem Lake soon enough."

Morrison stepped inside his room and swung the door shut behind him. He stepped into the dark and fumbled in his pocket for a match to strike and light the lantern.

The sound of laughter came from behind him and Jake Killrain said, "You'll get to Totem Lake sooner that you think," and Morrison was slammed in the side of the head with an ax handle. The darkness rushed up and engulfed him.

CHAPTER TWENTY ONE
On the Road to Totem Lake

It was still dark out when Morrison awoke in the back of a wagon being driven over rough ground. The wagon was rocking from side to side and when he opened his eyes he immediately looked into the face of Jake Killrain.

A lantern was lit and sitting off to the side of the wagon. It was wedged between two boxes to make sure it didn't fall over.

Killrain called to the driver, "Roy, our sleeping beauty is awake."

"Glad to hear it," Norton called back. "I was beginning to wonder if you'd hit him too dam hard with that ax handle."

"I didn't hit him near as hard as I wanted to," Killrain said.

Morrison tried to sit up and immediately found that his hands were tied behind him. He squirmed his way around and worked his way to a sitting position.

Killrain pointed Morrison's own pistol at him.

"Don't even think about trying to get away," Killrain told him. "I'd be more than happy to be the one to put a bullet through you."

Morrison smiled and looked right in Killrain's eyes. "I knew you were a low down dirty dog from the way you tried to fight me. But I would have guessed this kind of thing was too low even for you. I guess you'll be driving for a few more hours and then you'll shoot me in the head and dump me."

Norton heard that and laughed. "No, you're going to be fighting Night Knuckles. Dr. Abner ordered it and what Dr. Abner wants he gets."

Killrain told Morrison, "From what I hear about this Night Knuckles, you'd be better off if we did shoot you right now and get it over with. But that ain't going to happen. You see, I'm purely in this for the revenge. I'm keeping you alive just so I can see the look on your face when your bones are snapping."

CHAPTER TWENTY TWO
Stillwell

Shingi was up before the rising of the sun. Like every other morning she knocked on Morrison's door.

Usually it took about four raps then Morrison would be answering from inside that he was getting dressed and a few moments later he'd be opening the door ready to go to breakfast.

This morning the moment Shingi touched the door she knew the room was empty and that something was seriously wrong.

Shingi knocked anyway and as she knew would happen, no one answered. She went instantly down to the front desk and asked for a pass key.

The woman manning the front hotel desk was a frightened eyed red haired woman in her mid-twenties named Bonnie who always had serious man problems. Bonnie instantly assumed that Shingi was having the same kind of problems that she was always having and refused to give her a pass key.

Shingi, seeing that she was dealing with one of the dim-witted when Bonnie told her, "Darlin' don't you pay him no never mind. He'll be opening that door just as soon as he realizes what a good thing he's losing," went immediately to Barnum's room.

She rapped on his door.

Nothing.

She rapped again, this time louder and didn't stop knocking until she heard, "What-what-what-what? Stop beating on the door. You'll knock it down!"

A moment later Barnum threw the door open and had a fierce expression on his face because he was ready to chew somebody out for waking him.

The fierce expression melted as soon as he saw Shingi. He knew instinctively she wasn't the kind of person to do something like this lightly.

"What's the matter?" He asked.

"Buck L. Morrison is gone," Shingi stated. "He vanished during the night."

Barnum went back in and got dressed and reappeared a few minutes later. He held a ring of keys in his left hand.

On the way to Morrison's room Shingi told Barnum that they always had breakfast together and was always there when she knocked for him.

As they were walking, Barnum said to Shingi, "I want to put this delicately, but there really isn't any other way to ask something like this."

"Go ahead and ask," Shingi said.

"Is there any chance that Buck would have gone off with some other woman last night?"

Shingi answered without hesitation. "There is no chance of that at all," she said and her tone and conviction spoke more than words ever could.

Then they were at Morrison's door and Barnum knocked this time.

When he got no answer, Barnum used his pass key.

He opened the door and the two of them went in.

The bed was made and had not been slept in. Morrison's gun belt, pistol and rifle were gone.

On the floor in the middle of the room was a burned out match.

Shingi went and stood in front of the match. She looked down at it, then she looked straight out in front of herself, closing her eyes she inhaled.

Barnum didn't know what to make of this. He'd only once in his life met an Indian mystic who did something like this when that Indian had pulled a man with a gunshot wound back from the brink of death.

Seeing that had given Barnum a chill up his spine.

Seeing Shingi do this today gave Barnum a severe case of the goose bumps. Shingi came out of her mini-trance suddenly with an audible exhale and her eyes flashing open.

"He was standing here," Shingi said, "When someone struck him on the side of the head with something hard. He was told they are taking him to Totem Lake."

Barnum's mouth dropped open. He looked at Shingi with an expression of wide-eyed amazement.

"How do you know that?" Barnum asked.

"There is no how," Shingi told him. "I just know."

*   *   *

Barnum wasn't the type to blindly believe just anything. So while a part of him screamed that everything Shingi said was entirely true, another part of him was saying that until he had proof he wasn't going to believe that she could see things that everybody else couldn't. Because of that, he took Shingi and headed over to the training shed.

Clyde and Carl were there and were ready to start that days exercising.

"Where's Morrison?" Clyde asked. "He was going to show us some of his special moves today."

"He is gone," Shingi told the Hanson Brothers. "Men took him by force. They are going to Totem Lake."

"Well, let's go get him back," Carl said. "I'll bust somebody up-side the head they mess with Buck. He done taught me how to serve up a real good knuckle sandwich and I'm itching to try it out."

Barnum spoke, "Let's not jump to any conclusions here. All we really know is that Buck is missing. We don't know where he's gone."

"I know what I know," Shingi told Barnum.

She then asked the Hanson Brothers, "Where is Morrison's wagon? I thought he kept it back here."

"He does," Clyde answered. "But it was gone when we got here."

Shingi asked Barnum where Morrison kept Horse.

He pointed at the stable less than fifty yards away.

Shingi trailed by Barnum and the Hanson Brothers went in the stable.

Horse was there in his stall. Shingi went to him and stroked his muzzle. Horse snorted and licked her hand like an affectionate collie.

"They knew what Morrison's wagon looked like so they loaded him in and took it," Shingi told them. "In the dark all the horses look alike and they didn't dare light a lantern so they left Horse."

"There's no way to know this for sure," Barnum said.

"I am certain," Shingi answered.

"Let's go see the Sheriff then," Barnum told them. "We'll see if we can get together a search party or a posse or something."

*   *   *

The party of four went to the Sheriff's office. It was a dusty old place with cells that didn't have bars on the windows. Wanted posters that were at least ten years out of date were nailed up outside the front door.

The door to the Sheriff's office was unlocked so they went right on in.

It was almost nine o'clock in the morning. When they swung the door open and stepped inside the first thing they heard was loud snoring.

Barnum told Shingi to wait in the front office and he followed the snoring to an open jail cell where Sheriff Thomas Powell was stretched out on one of the cots sawing logs.

Barnum clapped his hands together four times. On the fourth clap the Sheriff's legs shot up into the air like he'd been punched in the gut.

"What in tarnation are you doing in here?" The Sheriff yelled at Barnum. He crawled out from underneath his one blanket and scratched his big pot belly. "Can't you leave a feller sleeping a little while longer?"

"The front door was open," Barnum told him. "That's why we came right on in."

"I locked it," the Sheriff mumbled as he wiped the sleep from his eyes.

"That don't make no never-mind," Barnum said. "We got a lawman job for you to do."

Sheriff Thomas Powell stood up off the cot. He swayed unsteadily. With his swaying since he was wearing red long johns from the neck on down he looked like a ripe tomato ready to fall off the vine.

"I'll be back in a minute," The Sheriff told Barnum and walked past him down a short hallway and through a door on the other side of the hall. He slammed the door shut behind him.

When he walked past Barnum the odor the Sheriff gave off made Barnum ask himself, *maybe I aught to offer him a complimentary bath at my place. It's a sure bet he ain't been bathing anywhere else.* But as soon as the door shut behind the Sheriff, Barnum though better of that. He figured any wash tub the Sheriff used would have to be thrown away as soon as he was done with it, and wash tubs don't come none too cheap.

A few minutes later Sheriff Thomas Powell came back out. He was dressed but he was still looking dirty and ragged. In his front office he met Barnum, Shingi and the Hanson Brothers.

"What do you people want?" The Sheriff spat out. "You come waking me up at the crack of dawn, this had better be important."

"This is far past the time when any man should be up," Shingi told the Sheriff.

"You shut your mouth Injun!" Sheriff Thomas snarled and pointed his finger in Shingi's face. "You'll speak when I tell you to."

Clyde slapped the Sheriff's hand out of the air in front of Shingi's face.

"You don't talk to her like that," Clyde shouted at the Sheriff. "You try to do that again I'll knock the teeth right out of your head!"

The Sheriff turned to Clyde. He yelled, "you trying to take up for this injun'? I'll lock you up so fast your head will spin."

Clyde yelled back, "Not after I knock you on your big fat ass you won't."

Barnum grabbed Clyde in a bear hug, spun him away from the Sheriff and walked with him to the wall. "This ain't helping nothin'," he told him. Then he came back to the Sheriff.

"We got a man missing and as you can see, him and the Indian gal are kind of important to these here boys," Barnum told the Sheriff.

"I don't care how important he is, or who the hell he is," Sheriff Thomas Powell yelled. "You come busting in here demanding that I do something when I don't have to do shit!"

Barnum put his hands up and said, "OK, I'm sorry for busting in on you like this. We're just worried about our friend. Let's everybody calm down and start over."

"That's right," Sheriff Thomas Powell told the entire room. "You all calm down, especially that idiot over there." He pointed at Clyde.

"I'll keep him corralled," Barnum said.

The Sheriff sat down behind his desk.

"Now, who is missing and how long has he been gone?" He asked.

"Buck L. Morrison wasn't in his room this morning when Shingi went to get him for breakfast," Barnum said. "We can't find him anywhere."

"So he's only been gone since this morning?" The Sheriff asked.

"He would never leave without telling us," Shingi said and the Sheriff gave her a mean look.

Sheriff Thomas Powell smiled then like he saw something that he liked. He said, "This Morrison is an adult. He can do as he pleases. If he's still missing in a week let me know and I'll ask around about him."

"So you ain't gonna do nothing," Carl said from across the room as him and Clyde glared at the Sheriff.

"That's right boy," the Sheriff said. "I ain't gonna do nothing. Now get the hell out of my office and quit bothering me."

There wasn't anything else to be done there so they all went back and walked out to the street. As soon as the last of them stepped out the door they heard the lock click behind them.

In the street Shingi turned to Barnum.

"I'll be stopping by The General Store to get supplies," she told him. "I'm taking Horse and going to Totem Lake."

"You don't know for certain that he was taken there," Barnum said.

"Yes, I do." Shingi told him. "I'm going there and I'll do whatever I have to, to get him back."

"I'm going too," Clyde said. "If Buck's in some trouble we'll take care of whoever put him in it."

"Don't count me out," Carl said. "Buck's my buddy too. We're going to go get him back."

"Well, I can't go," Barnum told them. "I got too many business dealings to take care of to just up and be off. Get what you need from the store and charge it to me. You can pay me back later."

It was then that Shingi told Clyde, Carl and Barnum about her vision about the evil thing in Totem Lake and what she expected to be waiting for them.

"That don't change a thing," Clyde said. "I figure I'm a big enough boy to stomp on a few spiders."

Carl said, "I'll just put on my bug crunchin' boots and go to town on them critters."

Barnum looked at the three of them.

"I still got my business to run," he said and walked away.

*   *   *

The Hanson Brothers got their horses and their rifles and ammo. Shingi got Horse and they stocked up at The General Store. Then they hit the trail heading to Totem Lake.

CHAPTER TWENTY THREE
Totem Lake

Stephen Caldwell worked for The Seattle Times as its sports reporter. Things had been going slow for him lately, just not much sports to report on. Then the telegraph came in requesting a reporter from the Seattle Times to be present for the next fight of the "Greatest Bare-Knuckle Two Fisted Warrior the World Has Ever Seen: Night Knuckles."

The telegram said someone named Dr. Abner was paying all the expenses for a Seattle Times reporter to witness Night Knuckles destroy his next opponent.

When the paper's managing editor offered the assignment to Stephen he jumped at it. *This is going to be a paid vacation, is what he immediately thought, a month or so away from the boss looking over my shoulder, a month to interview any local celebrities and maybe bed a few of the local star struck bar flies.*

A paid vacation!

Stephen took the stage to Totem Lake and arrived around noon. That was when his nightmare began.

He was the only passenger on the stage when it arrived in Totem Lake and when it drove away he felt very lonely. The streets were empty. Everything, even the saloons were closed.

Stephen started to walk toward what looked like a hotel when a small man dressed all in black wearing a black hat came out of the door of that building.

As the man in black approached him Stephen felt his own will melt away until the man was standing directly in front of him and held his gaze with eyes that glowed from beneath the brim of his black hat.

Without being told Stephen knew that this man was Dr. Abner.

Abner spoke. "Look to the crossroads," he said and pointed to the open square where the streets met.

There were four posts driven into the ground marking off a square.

"That is where Night Knuckles will defeat his next challenger and we will move a step closer to taking the Championship of the World," Abner said. "You will be our personal voice to the newspapers of the world. You will inform the world about the greatest warrior who ever lived and make challenges to all the top fighters. Your life, from this moment forward, is for that purpose only."

He was then ordered to take a room at Hillarie's House of Pleasure, which he did. But he never partook of the pleasures of the women who lived at the house.

Stephen Caldwell ate when food was brought to him, slept and bathed as was needed and he thought of nothing else than how to promote the fighting career of Night Knuckles.

To push Night Knuckles toward the World Title was all that Stephen Caldwell thought about. It was all he lived for.

CHAPTER TWENTY FOUR
On the Road to Totem Lake

Three days into the journey back Roy Norton sat in front of a small campfire wolfing down a dinner of jerked beef and beans that they took out of Morrison's wagon. Morrison sat on the other side of the fire slowly eating his meal and Jake Killrain sat some distance behind him with a six-shooter in his left hand and a spoon in his right.

Killrain shoveled a few spoonful's of beans into his mouth then bit off a strip of the dried beef. He grimaced.

"This stuff tastes like dried dog dick," Killrain said.

"You aught to know," Morrison told him.

"What's that supposed to mean?" Killrain asked.

Morrison laughed at him.

"He just said that you eat dog dick," Norton said.

"Is that so?" Killrain asked.

"That's exactly so," Morrison told him.

"You won't be laughing if I grab that ax handle and commence to raising some more knots on your head to go with that first one I gave you." Killrain said.

"You ain't got the guts to try it with my hands untied." Morrison told him.

Killrain glared at Morrison.

"Don't let him bait you," Norton said. "We'll be in Totem Lake soon. Then you'll get to watch his bones break."

Roy ate the rest of his meal as quick as he could. Then with Killrain holding the pistol on Morrison he tied his hands behind him.

Killrain took first watch. He let Norton sleep for two hours before they switched out and Killrain slept for two hours.

After that they were rolling again, not riding hard and fast but keeping up a constant pace.

In two days Norton knew they would be back in Totem Lake. They would turn Morrison over to Dr. Abner to be put in the ring with Night Knuckles.

Then Norton was hoping that Dr. Abner would just let him go. If he didn't Roy didn't know what he would do. He sure didn't want to live the rest of his life like this. If he had to live like this, being Dr. Abner's personal puppet, then he didn't want to live at all.

CHAPTER TWENTY FIVE
On the Road to Totem Lake

The Hanson Brothers sat before their campfire slowly turning their spitted rabbit. Grease dripped from the meat into the flames and sizzled. They had ridden long and hard the last three days following the trail from Morrison's wagon that they'd picked up just outside Stillwell. They were tired.

They knew they would arrive in Totem Lake after Morrison and his two abductors got there, but not long afterward, six hours at the very most.

Shingi sat across the fire from them. She sat in a cross legged Indian squat with her hands resting upon her knees. Her eyes were closed. She breathed evenly and deeply like someone who was sleeping but the Hanson Brothers knew she was not asleep.

When she first sat down Shingi asked Carl and Clyde to be very quiet so she could concentrate.

Because of that Carl now leaned over to Clyde and whispered, "I'll take the first watch. You go catch some sleep and I'll wake you in about three hours."

Clyde didn't need to be told this twice. He grunted, stood up, and turned around to go get his bed roll and almost ran right into Barnum who was leading a fine looking sleek black horse into the camp.

"You aught to be more watchful out here in the countryside," Barnum told him. "If I'd have been someone with something against you, you could both be dead by now."

Clyde put a finger to his lips and shushed Barnum saying, "We need to be a little quiet. Shingi's talking to her ancestors or something."

"Oh," Barnum said.

"But it is good to see you," Clyde told him and went and got his bed roll and stretched out.

Barnum sat down beside Carl who took a bite of the still cooking rabbit and offered him some.

"No thanks," Barnum told him. "I bought me a supply of smoked sausages and have been eating them directly from the saddle bag as I was riding."

"What are you doing here?" Carl asked Barnum.

"Well, after you boys and Shingi rode out I got to thinking about that story that Shingi told about that big spider and the little ones eating all the people in Totem Lake and even though it does seem real far-fetched to me, if something happened to the three of you, I'd never feel right about it. I'm here to protect you boy," Barnum said and slapped Carl on the back.

"Yeah, well if you ain't too good at that," Carl answered. "I guess we'll be protecting you."

*　　*　　*

Shingi floated in the half space between the world of the living and the world of the dead. She floated in the eternal darkness that is the borderland between two universes.

Shingi called out, "Oh Great Spirit of the Earth I seek your guidance and I seek the courage to face the evil that waits in the white man's town of Totem Lake."

Only silence answered her.

Shingi repeated the same call and after the second time also received only silence.

Now Shingi did something that she had never done before. She used her secret language. Inside every great shaman there is a language that has never been spoken in either the world of the living or the world of the dead.

It is the language of the Nothingness of the Spaces Between. It is a language that she had never been taught. The words had been in her head since the day she was born, and perhaps before then.

In this unknown secret language Shingi chanted out a plea for help in defeating the evil thing.

This time the Spirit of the Earth answered.

"In the battle between good and evil where the fate of all mankind will be determined for the next millennia we are only observers. We are only to watch and take no part.

"But there is one of the Dark Gods, who men in other lands called Elder Gods who has been influencing the events in Totem Lake.

"Before the contest begins I will remove this Dark God and his influence over events will stop. The living will then have free will. But the dead will still be hungry pawns."

Shingi thought on this for a moment then said, "You have shown me many visions of things in the past. Can you show me who will survive?"

The Great Spirit of the Earth spoke again.

"The visions I showed you before were of things which had been or might be. The events in Totem Lake are a test to determine who is worthy to have dominion over the Earth; the forces of darkness or the forces of light.

"Who survives is not important, only if you prove yourselves worthy."

Then she found herself sitting back in front of the fire. Shingi felt incredibly tired, like the weight of the entire world rested on her shoulders and in a way she figured it did.

When Barnum saw her eyes open he came over to her. "How are you doing?" He asked.

"As well as can be expected for someone who is going into a fight where all of us may die," Shingi told him. "You do understand that every single one of us may not leave Totem Lake alive."

"I understand that you know that something very bad is waiting for us," Barnum told her. "Whatever it is, we'll all meet it together."

FINAL CONFRONTATION
TOTEM LAKE
11:45 PM

The torches at the crossroads were burning throwing out blazing yellow and red light across the square. Ropes had been drawn tight and tied off between posts marking off the square battle ground and now Sheriff Matt Jackson and Deputy Don Carson with guns in their hands emerged from the Jail House with Buck L. Morrison walking in front of them.

Six hours before Dr. Abner showed up at the Jail House along with two other men who were shoving Morrison in front of them with his hands bound behind his back.

Dr. Abner spoke slowly and clearly to the Sheriff and his Deputy, "You will keep this man in your jail cell until eleven forty-five tonight when you will walk him out to the ring where he will fight Night Knuckles. Sheriff, you will referee. Do you understand?"

"Yes, I understand," Sheriff Matt Jackson said as though he was half asleep.

Then the Sheriff did exactly as Dr. Abner had told him, even though his inner thoughts screamed for him not to.

The Sheriff hated what he was doing but he could not stop himself. It was as though somebody else was inside his skin and he was only an observer to what his body was doing.

It took an intense act of will and so much pain lanced through his head that tears ran down his cheeks but while walking Morrison to the ring the Sheriff managed to speak words that were his own and not ones that had been fed to him. His words were choked off and harsh like the last gasp of a dying man as he said, "I'm sorry. This is wrong. Somehow, Abner controls us."

Morrison saw the tears on the man's face. He saw the strain and the pain that forcing those words out caused the Sheriff and he believed that the Sheriff and the Deputy had no choice in what they were doing.

"Don't worry about it," Morrison told the two lawmen. "I'm going to put this big bastard on his ass in the dirt. Then we can see what Abner says about that."

Unlike the last time that a prizefight was held in the crossroads there were only three men besides Morrison and the lawmen that stood outside the ropes to watch. They were the reporter from The Seattle Times, Stephen Caldwell, Roy Norton, and Jake Killrain.

Except for them, the streets were empty.

But from the shadows of the alleyways and the darkness between the buildings of Totem Lake the majority of the citizens of the town waited.

* * *

It was a clear dark night when Shingi and Barnum and the Hanson Brothers rode across the line separating the wild countryside from the town of Totem Lake. The instant that they crossed over into what could be called a street they felt a difference in the air.

There was a bone tingling chill on the breeze. Their horses whinnied and snorted nervously. The air felt strangely heavy. There was a feeling in all of them like their jaw teeth were vibrating. Electricity crackled in the atmosphere around the entire town of Totem Lake.

Before now they had been riding smoothly to conserve their horse's strength so they could cover the most distance over the longest period of time.

Now, suddenly Shingi spurred her mount forward and yelled, "Move!"

All four of the horses shot forward at a break neck pace.

A bolt of lightning crashed to the ground right in the center of where their horses were a moment earlier exploding on impact sending a shower of dirt into the air.

The riders sent their horses down the street deep into Totem Lake at a mad gallop as lightning bolts crashed down to the street around them.

*   *   *

Morrison was already in the ring, leaning up against one of the posts with the Sheriff in ring center as Night Knuckles stepped over the top rope when the first lightning bolt crashed to the ground to be followed closely behind by several others.

Dr. Abner for once in the last few hundred years of his existence was surprised. He looked up to the sky and was treated to a light display the likes of which had never been seen before upon the North American Continent.

In a clear sky, where there was a crescent moon and stars twinkling, lightning bolts flew back and forth in a whirlwind of rage like some kind of an insane electrical duel was being fought.

And that's exactly what was happening. To the extreme north and to the extreme south enormous dark beings were seen towering over the horizons. They were only seen when the lightning bolts struck home and showed the outline of their forms.

The duel between these dark beings did not last long. They sent bolts flashing back and forth faster than the humans could even blink until the one from the north screamed out a sound that made the ground vibrate like an Earthquake.

Then he was gone, vanished into nothingness, the other dark being disappeared a moment later. His task had been completed.

Roy Norton who had been standing to the left of Dr. Abner beside Jake Killrain suddenly grabbed his head.

"The pain is gone!" He yelled and turning he ran down the street.

Jake Killrain looked at the retreating figure of Roy Norton and yelled after him, "Where the hell you going? You're going to miss a dam good fight!"

Stephen Caldwell sports reporter for The Seattle Times backed away from his spot next to the ropes shaking his head like somebody suddenly awakening from a drunken sleep. He looked at Dr. Abner then threw away the notebook and pen he held in his hands. Caldwell turned and bolted down the street running in the same direction that Roy Norton ran in.

Dr. Abner shouted to his fighter, "Get him now! End it fast!"

Night Knuckles charged at Morrison.

*   *   *

When the first lightning bolt crashed to the ground aimed at them and then the lightning started being shot back and forth across the sky Shingi knew that the battle between the Gods was taking place.

When they were not blasted into flaming ruin and made it to ringside Shingi knew that the Great Spirit of the Earth had won that struggle.

But now Morrison was in the fight of his life and this was a fight that could not be interfered with. This contest, as much as if they survived, would determine whether the Earth would be ruled by darkness or light.

*   *   *

Night Knuckles charged in swinging haymakers as he came.

The Sheriff jumped in front of him yelling, "Hold it right there! I'm the referee and I've got to lay down some rules for you to follow."

Night Knuckles swatted him out of the way like he was a child's rag doll and Sheriff Matt Jackson went sliding to the ropes where he laid dazed with blood flowing from his nose.

Shingi standing outside the ropes locked eyes with Dr. Abner. Across the distance between them Abner tried to send out his will to control this woman who he knew at first sight was a powerful Shaman native to this land.

He tried to reach inside Shingi's mind, to grab hold of it, to squeeze it, and mold it to his will.

Nothing happened.

Dr. Abner did not know why but a large chunk of his power had been taken away from him.

Shingi shouted to the Sheriff, who crawled dazed from between the ropes, his Deputy and the others with her, "All is equal now. This duel must be fought without our help!"

And a duel to the death is exactly what it was.

Night Knuckles came in swinging and Morrison slipped to the side stepping around him until Night Knuckles was out of position and off balance by one of his huge misses. Then Morrison stepped forward and scored with a left jab to the stomach, a left hook to the ribs and an overhand right to the tip of Night Knuckles nose.

The right jarred Night Knuckles backward a step.

Morrison spun away keeping a close eye on his opponent at all times.

Blood came from Night Knuckles nose. He reached up and touched it smearing some on his fingers. When Night Knuckles looked at the blood on his hand an intense bulging-eyed look of surprise came over his face.

Dr. Abner yelled at Night Knuckles from ringside. "You are not an immortal now. Kill him! If you lose, you go back to being the dirt and bones that I raised from the dead!"

Night Knuckles charged in again and almost overwhelmed Morrison with the pure ferocity of his attack. He swung blows at Morrison that would have brought down the walls of buildings if they had landed.

One wild right hook clipped Morrison on the left shoulder and he found out in that moment that he couldn't afford to be hit twice. That one punch made his arm go numb all the way down to his fingers.

Morrison retreated until he felt the feeling come back into his arm. Then he started using it again to land stinging straight jabs to Night Knuckles nose and stomach. He occasionally mixed in a quick right.

The problem was the punches Morrison landed seemed to have almost no effect as far as hurting Night Knuckles. Night Knuckles seemed to be impervious to pain.

In his first life before being resurrected Night Knuckles had been the greatest Viking warrior who had ever lived. His name had been Ragnar and he led his Vikings in raids all along the English coast and deep into the heart of the European continent.

Ragnar left such a bloody trail behind him that his name became legend. When he raided villages he took everything of value, burned the houses to the ground and left no one, men, women or children alive.

Night Knuckles remembered those days now. In those days he had fought in a berserker's cold fury where only the death of his opponent mattered.

He fought Buck L. Morrison like that.

Morrison was beginning to feel a little bit of fatigue when he got close to Night Knuckles and was grabbed and thrown to the ground.

Being used to having some rules Morrison almost relaxed when he hit the dirt. Going down meant a thirty second rest period in the London Prize Ring Rules.

He was glad he didn't relax though when Night Knuckles ran at him and tried to stomp him into the Earth.

Morrison rolled away from the big man's stomp that vibrated the ground knowing if that stomp had landed his head would have been crushed. From the dirt he chambered a kick up and into Night Knuckles gonads.

Night Knuckles grunted bending over slightly at the waist and backed up.

Morrison got to his feet and told Night Knuckles, "That got your attention now didn't it! Now all your children will be born with short necks."

Then it occurred to him that since Night Knuckles wasn't following any rules, it would be crazy for him to even attempt to.

Morrison's hands were getting sore from the hard punches he was landing. He had raised some marks on Night Knuckles head but Morrison was beginning to wonder if he was hurting his hands worse than he was hurting Night Knuckle's head.

Night Knuckles charged in again and instead of slipping off to the left like Morrison usually did, this time he slid out to the right side.

When Night Knuckles missed a huge right hook, he left his entire left leg exposed.

On instinct Morrison stepped forward and slammed a hard kick into Night Knuckles thigh right above his knee.

The kick buckled his leg and Night Knuckles halted his forward progress. A pained expression came over his face.

Morrison stepped to the right and nailed the same leg with another kick.

*   *   *

Roy Norton ran like a deer. Never had he wanted to escape any place as fast as what he wanted to get away from Totem Lake. Since he showed up in this town his life had become the waking nightmare of being the mind controlled puppet of an ugly little troll of a man.

He was going to run right on out of there. Run all the way out into the country, live off the land and if he had to, walk to the next town. Roy didn't care where he went, just so long as he put a lot of distance between himself and Dr. Abner.

Norton didn't know what had happened to break Abner's power over him and he didn't really care. He just wanted to get the hell out of Totem Lake before Dr. Abner got the chance to crawl inside his head again.

Roy got about a block and a half away from the crossroads when he had to slow down and take a breath. He'd run at full tilt and all his wind was gone. He slowed to a walk and on trembling legs moved on and looked around him.

The streets were dark and deserted. Not one lamp burned in any window. The weak silver light of the crescent moon shined down on everything.

The silence was frightening.

Off to the left hand side was a line of closed and boarded-up shops. Between two of those shops the silvery moonlight shone Earthward in a diagonal line.

Someone stepped out of the shadows. The soft silvery light shined across them from the neck on down. The face was left in darkness.

The figure that stepped out was a woman, completely naked. She beckoned to Roy with her hands to come closer. Looking at her, Roy thought he recognized the rounded breasts and the flat stomach as belonging to one of

126

the girls that he rented at Hillarie's House of Pleasure on one of his other visits to Totem Lake.

What was her name? Roy thought. Oh yeah, she's named Rhonda. Yeah, and she'd been an athletic little thing too, with some strange foreign accent that made me get real hot for her.

Someone else stepped out of the shadows beside her. A tall thin man dressed in a black suit and stove pipe hat. And someone else stepped out beside him, a teenage boy in a white shirt with black oily stains on it.

What the hell is this? Roy asked himself. Even if I did want to stop for a bit of fun in the dark I ain't the kind of guy who goes in for making it a family affair.

Rhonda's arms were stuck straight out in front of her waving for Roy to come to her. She stepped fully into the light.

Rhonda had the same cute pixy face that Roy remembered, at least on the left side of her head she did. On the right side of her face chunks had been bitten out and her right eye hung by tendons down to the raggedy chopped meat-hole that made up her left cheek.

"Oh shit!" Roy shouted stumbling backward as all three of them darted out from between the buildings and knocked him off his feet to the ground.

They climbed up on top of Roy as he screamed, "Get off of me!" and fought with the desperation of a madman. But although he punched and kicked and clawed they were more viscous than he was.

The three things from the pitch blackness bit chunks out of Roy Norton anywhere they could get their teeth on him. They snapped and bit at him like rabid dogs until Roy stopped fighting and until he lay still beneath them.

Then they fed upon Roy Norton.

*   *   *

Stephen Caldwell ran in the same direction Roy went, figuring Roy must know a faster way out of town than he did since he didn't know this town at all. Stephen was not in as good a physical shape as Roy so he tired faster and stopped to rest at least fifty yards before Roy did.

He was walking forward building steam for his next run when he witnessed the attack on Roy Norton.

The pure savagery of the blood hungry creatures that only looked like people froze Stephen in his tracks. He stayed frozen until the teenage boy looked up from his meal and looked square into Stephen's eyes. The boy's eyes were not human. They were the eyes of a predator. The boy looked at Stephen the same way a tiger looks at a gazelle gauging whether or not the prey he spotted was fast enough to get away.

Stephen backed away from the scene in front of him and turned to run in the same direction that he came from. He found standing in his way, walking slowly and carefully so as to not gain his attention, was four more of these walking dead people.

Stephen could see that they had to be dead. One of them was slit right up the middle and was missing his internal organs like he'd woke up in the middle of his own autopsy.

Stephen turned back just in time to see the boy springing at him. He dodged the boy and ran diagonally across the street. The four took up the chase along with the boy.

Stephen screamed at the five as he ran, "Leave me alone! What the hell do you want?" When he knew full well that what they wanted was a meal with him as the entrée.

He ran across the street and two more of these shambling nightmares came out of the shadows between the buildings in front of him.

Stephen veered to the left and more of these people who should be in their graves came from the alleyways and the shadows running toward him seeking his flesh.

He dodged past the first line of ghouls in the street and saw ahead of him that more of them were coming out of the shadows. The street ahead was filling with the dead citizens of Totem Lake.

Stephen knew there was no way he was going to make it through that street so he darted into the darkness between McMann's Shoe Store and The Happy Buns Bakery and that was when he was brought down.

A little girl perhaps ten years old, leaped out from beside the corner of McMann's Shoe Store and tackled Stephen by grabbing him around the ankles. Then three more of the slobbering dead was on his back forcing him to the ground.

Stephen fought as they bit and tore at him and the one thought that was in his mind was, *Oh God, please get this over with fast.*

* * *

Night Knuckles didn't like those leg kicks one bit. He howled at Morrison some kind of a weird shrill ear-splitting war cry that was designed to freeze an opponent in terror.

All it did to Morrison was to make him realize he couldn't play with this boy at all. He knew that this Night Knuckles dude was only there for one reason, to kill him.

Morrison had found a formula that worked good in this fight with moving right and throwing right leg kicks to Night Knuckles thigh so he kept at it. He landed two more hurtful kicks before he was sliding past the ropes and was tripped by someone on the outside sticking his foot in under the bottom rope.

He tripped and fell backward and a glance showed him the grinning face of Jake Killrain leering at him from outside the ring.

Night Knuckles saw the opportunity and took it, leaping onto Morrison and clubbing down with his right fist in a hammer like fashion.

The first blow landed on the side of Morrison's head making stars explode all around him. Then when Night Knuckles drew back to deliver another one, Morrison grabbed him and jerked his head down while bringing his own head up and butted Night Knuckles in the nose.

Night Knuckles screamed out in pain and got both of his hands on Morrison's neck and started to squeeze. His grip was like a hydraulic press and after one second of that pressure Morrison decided he'd had enough of that.

I'm sending this bastard to hell! He thought.

Morrison reached up and poked both of his thumbs into Night Knuckles eyes and jammed them in as far as they would go. Then Morrison jerked to the side and ripped Night Knuckles eyes from the sockets. Grasping the two orbs in his hands still connected by nerve tissue he brought the two eyes in front of his own face and somehow felt that Night Knuckles could still see him through those disconnected eyeballs so he squeezed his hands shut and squished the fluid out of Night Knuckles eyes. The eye-sap spurted from between his fingers.

The scream that Night Knuckles screeched out was more animal than human. He let go and stumbled blindly around the ring. Then he collapsed to the dirt and moved no more.

Morrison jumped up holding the squashed eyeballs in his hands and looked at Dr. Abner and shouted at him, "You want to hear a rhyme? Here's one for you. Buck L. Morrison with a shout, poked Night Knuckles eyeballs out. Squeezed them hard until they popped, now's about the time that this shit stopped!"

He threw the crushed eyes at Dr. Abner and they bounced off his chest and fell to the dirt.

The Sheriff, now fully recovered and standing at the side of the ring looked at Night Knuckles.

"You can count over him if you want to," Morrison told the Sheriff. "But I doubt he's going to be getting up and coming back for more."

He climbed out through the ropes and greeted Shingi, Barnum and the Hanson Brothers. "Just another night at the office," He told them.

Dr. Abner shouted, "This is not over!"

"I think it is," Morrison yelled back.

Sheriff Matt Jackson along with Deputy Don Carson went and congratulated Morrison on his victory.

Jake Killrain watched Dr. Abner as he spread his arms and shouted, "Come to me, come to me my children of the night. Come and kill them all!"

They saw behind him appearing out of the darkness, out of the shadowy places into the silvery moonlight, misshapen people, people missing limbs and pieces of their faces. These things that should be dead and buried came at Dr. Abner's command.

At first, only a few appeared out of the misty night. But in only a couple of seconds those few were joined by dozens and then too many to count came lumbering down the road in the direction that Dr. Abner pointed.

The first things that got spooked were the horses. With the first sight of the walking dead they pulled loose from where they were tied and dashed off down the road.

Morrison looked at the gathering swarm of shambling creatures coming toward them and said, "You know, I could be wrong about this here being over with."

The Deputy pulled his six-shooter.

"I think we should all head for the Jail House," He said, and looking around they saw that dark shapes were coming toward them from all four sides of the cross roads.

They backed away from the ring as one group and just before the seven of them turned to run to the Jail House the corpse of Night Knuckles burst into flame where it lay in the dirt.

The body of the Ancient Viking Warrior burned with an unnatural intensity giving off a white hot light they had to shield their eyes from that lasted only about five seconds then died to nothing leaving smoking ashes where Night Knuckles had been.

A sudden gust blew up seemingly out of nowhere, and scattered the ashes that was Night Knuckles to the four winds. After but a few moments it was as though he never existed.

Deputy Don Carson swung his six-shooter around and brought it up to take a shot at Dr. Abner.

He fired and missed.

Dr. Abner's hand flew up in front of him. Then he flicked his fingers out like he was flinging water from a wet hand.

Like he was punched in the chest by an enormous fist, the Deputy was knocked flying off his feet through the air a good thirty feet and crashed into the wall beside the front Jail House door.

Now they could hear the moaning of the zombies as they converged on the living people at the cross roads.

I call these things zombies because that's the only word that I can think of to describe what they were. These things were dead. They ate people and looked ugly as hell. I'm not going to get technical about it. Being dead and ugly and hungry makes them zombies to me.

The Sheriff and Morrison's group ran to where the Deputy lay in a crumpled heap outside the Jail house and just before they got to him three of the living dead came around the corner of the building and leaped on him.

Barnum got there first. Like Clyde and Carl he was carrying his rifle with him. He clubbed one of the things in the head with his rifle butt and knocked it away. Another one he shot in the chest. The bullet drove it up against the wall where it slid to the ground leaving a black stain behind it.

The last one was dragged away and thrown off by the Hanson Brothers who shot it about six times and made it dance a jig.

Shingi took a good close look at the deputy who was starting to moan and regain consciousness. She saw that he was bit deep on the left shoulder but it was not a serious wound.

"Get him inside," Shingi told the others and Morrison grabbed one of Don Carson's arms and hoisted him up. Somebody else grabbed the Deputy's other arm to carry him through the door and Morrison saw that it was Jake Killrain who was helping out.

Morrison told him, "Don't you be thinking this takes you off the hook. You're a long way from there!"

Shingi went with them as they carried Don Carson inside.

The Sheriff had drawn his six-shooter while running. He used it when he saw the zombie that Barnum shot in the chest sit up and start to climb to its feet. Sheriff Matt Jackson shot the zombie that looked uncannily like a harmless old lady right through the side of the head.

This time she went down and stayed down.

The Hanson Brothers were having a hell of a time with their zombie. The one they'd shot at least six times looked something like a bank teller. He seemed to have more life in him now than when he was alive, because every time he hit the dirt from their bullets he popped right back up like a jack-in-the-box and came right back after them.

"Shoot him in the head!" Sheriff Matt Jackson yelled at them and Barnum took careful aim to do just that.

That was when Barnum felt a hot pain in his ankle and looked down to see that the teenage boy zombie that he'd clubbed in the head had fastened his teeth to his ankle and was clamping down for all he was worth.

Barnum ignored the teenage biter and squeezed off a shot to the forehead to drop the bank teller to his back. Then he chambered another round into his Winchester and splattered the teen zombie's brains all over his pants leg and the wall.

Barnum had to pry the lad's teeth loose from his leg with the barrel of his rifle.

The Hanson Brothers went in through the door followed closely by the limping Barnum.

The walking dead were getting thick outside as Sheriff Matt Jackson dropped two more of them before he stepped in through the door. He looked back out scanning the cross roads at the gathering of animated corpses coming to tear him and the others inside the Jail House to pieces and thought, I stayed here to protect you. Well, the least I can do now is send as many of you to hell as I can.

The Sheriff slammed the door shut and set the dead bolt. To make extra sure it was secure he grabbed a thick wooden chair and wedged it tight underneath the door knob. Anyone trying to force that door inward would actually be wedging the chair tighter.

Morrison and Killrain laid Don Carson on one of the cots in a jail cell. He had looked like he was going to come around but now he just moaned and his head rocked from side to side like he was in some real serious pain.

Shingi asked the Sheriff if he had any bandages.

He said he didn't but that she was welcome to get one of his shirts from his room and tear it to shreds.

This, she did.

As Shingi was bandaging the Deputy's wounds, Killrain started trying to be friendly with Morrison by telling him, "That was some really good fighting you did out there. That Night Knuckles was a tough son-of-a-bitch."

"Yeah he was," Morrison answered. "Now he's well done too."

When Shingi was done with the Deputy she stood in front of Killrain who towered over her.

"Are you one of the men who brought Buck L. Morrison here by force?" She asked him.

Killrain answered, "Yes ma'am I am and I am rightfully sorry for doing that. Now I see that it was a wrong thing to do. I was looking for a little revenge, when I should have just figured he beat me fair and square."

Shingi kneed Killrain in the crotch. He grunted and bent over. She hit him as hard as she could in the stomach knocking the wind from his lungs and he went to his knees.

"Saying you are sorry does not change a thing," Shingi told him and stormed out of the jail cell and went to tend to Barnum's bite wound.

Sheriff Matt Jackson shouted to the Hanson Bothers, "Come in here boys and give me a hand."

He motioned for them to join him at a closet that was across from the jail cells. Inside the closet standing up was somewhere around ten rifles and shotguns. There was a pile of hand guns laying on the floor and dozens of boxes of ammunition.

"Stack these over on the desk so we can get at them quick," The Sheriff said.

Glass was heard breaking in the window in Matt Jackson's bedroom.

The Sheriff pointed at the guns and told the boys, "I have a feeling we're going to need all of these. If things get really bad there's an old tunnel underneath the floor boards in the cell where Don is. It's not something that I liked to spread around but years before I was here, some prisoners escaped that way."

Clyde and Carl piled the weapons and ammo on the Sheriff's desk. Then at his instruction they started loading every weapon with as many bullets as they would hold. Before the Hanson's were done the window in the wall behind the Sheriff's desk shattered inward and hands reached through the bars and tore down the blinds.

Carl grabbed up a rifle and pointed it at a drooling dead man trying to squeeze through the bars.

The Sheriff shouted at him, "Make it a head shot. That seems to stop them in their tracks."

Carl took aim and blasted a ragged hole right between the guy's eyes. He fell away and was immediately replaced be two of the living dead who jerked and tugged at the bars trying to get inside.

The Sheriff told the Hanson Brothers, "Aim careful. We don't have an unlimited supply of bullets and I sure as hell don't want to find out what happens when we run out."

Both of the brothers had rifles now and started picking off the hungry dead as they came to the windows trying to tear the bars loose with their bare hands.

Shingi was working on Barnum and didn't like what she was seeing. She bandaged the bite and it wasn't bleeding anymore but Barnum was alternating between having chills and running a raging fever

"Jesus Christ!" Patrick Barnum told her. "One minute I'm burning up, then the next I feel like I'm on a block of ice. What the hell did that guy have that bit me? Do you think he might have had rabies?"

"Rabies wouldn't do anything this fast," Shingi told him. "We'll hold out and get you to a good doctor at sun up."

The window in the jail cell that Don Carson was in shattered and the creatures attacked those bars with a vengeance.

Morrison and Killrain ran into the main room and without a word grabbed two rifles and went back toward the jail cell.

The Sheriff started to say something to them and Morrison tossed back over his shoulder, "Yeah, we know. Shoot them in the head!"

There followed after that a period of time, and it was impossible to know how long it was with everything happening so fast, that Morrison and Killrain kept shooting the zombies out of the barred jail cell window and Carl and Clyde kept blasting holes in the heads of the dead citizens of Totem Lake and Sheriff Matt Jackson reloaded the rifles as they were emptied while Shingi tended to the two wounded men as well as she could.

Shingi gave Barnum a bottle of the Sheriff's rot gut whiskey to help ease the pain as his symptoms got steadily worse. She had given up the Deputy for dead a few minutes earlier.

While checking on him and trying to force a little bit of water between his lips Deputy Don Carson went suddenly stiff, what color was still in his face drained away to a pasty white, then he shook violently and exhaled a rattling last breath and went limp on the cot.

Shingi pulled the blanket up over his face and asked the Great Spirit of the Earth to protect the Deputy's Spirit on its journey to its next life and went back to Barnum.

That was when Deputy Don Cason threw his blanket off and lurched to his feet. He charged Morrison and Killrain and with all the shooting going on they didn't see him until he rammed into the two of them.

Morrison flew sideways and slammed into Killrain who flying off his feet cracked his head hard against the wall.

Killrain went down and out and the Deputy climbed on top of Morrison trying to force his teeth down onto Morrison's throat. Morrison had both hands around Don Carson's neck but choking him wasn't doing any good since the Deputy wasn't breathing anyway.

That was when Clyde Hanson came running into the room and did a flying tackle knocking the zombie that Don Carson had become off Morrison.

Clyde rolled to the side away from Don Carson. When Clyde got to his knees Carson jumped on top of him knocking him to his back. When Carson lunged down with his mouth wide open to put the bite on Clyde, Clyde straight armed his face away from him and he was bit on the palm. Clyde then straightened his legs out and flipped the Deputy up, over, and out the door of the cell and into the main room.

The Sheriff met his Deputy in the main room and gave him a thunderous right hook to the side of the head that knocked Carson flying from his feet. As soon as he hit the floor Don Carson instantly started to get up. Sheriff Matt Jackson grabbed Don Carson by the hair of the head and forced his head back. He took a moment to look into the lifeless eyes and snapping teeth of his former friend. He drew his six-shooter.

The Sheriff spoke to him. "Son, you were a hell of a good Deputy and I want to thank you for a lot of years of friendship. I don't think you're still in there, but if you are, I'm sorry."

He jammed the barrel of his pistol in Don Carson's mouth and fired blowing the back of his head all over the wall behind him.

Patrick Barnum was standing up while being racked by chills and sweats. He watched everything that had happened with the Deputy. When Shingi was called to treat Clyde's bite wound and check out Killrain he walked over to where the Sheriff was back to reloading the rifles that Carl was emptying into the faces of the walking dead.

"I'm going to end up just like him," Barnum told Matt Jackson and pointed to the corpse of Don Carson. "I can feel my muscles tightening up. I'm not even sure if my heart beats anymore. I don't even need to breath. I just suck air in so I can speak to you. And I can smell your blood too. It smells good, just like a big juicy steak and I'm feeling like I ain't ate in about a month.

"Sheriff, I don't want to try to eat my own friends. Shoot me in the head right now and get it over with."

Matt Jackson looked hard at Barnum.

"I'll keep a close eye on you," he told him. "If you change suddenly, I'll do that."

"There might not be time then," Barnum told the Sheriff.

He walked over and picked up his rifle from the floor and then walked to the front door.

"Tell them I said good-bye," Patrick Barnum shouted and kicked the chair out from under the door knob, undid the dead bolt and jerking the door open he stepped outside.

Barnum was met by two female zombies, one a blond and one a brunette, that looked like dead whores from Hillarie's House of Pleasure since both of them were in black and red see through night gowns.

"Sorry ladies," Barnum told the pair. "Too bad you didn't greet me dressed like this about a month ago. We'd of had a real good time. It's a little too late now."

He shot the blond through the left eye and when the brunette charged him he knocked her to the ground with his rifle butt and shot her in the back of the head when she started to rise.

There was a crowd of zombies milling around in front of the jail house and Barnum walked toward them firing as he went.

The Sheriff was watching all this in shocked fascination from the open door until Morrison shoved him to the side just in time to see the swarm of zombies close in a circle around Barnum.

Barnum screamed as they got their hands on him and tore and bit at him. He shot as many as he could and clubbed with the butt of his Winchester the ones too close to shoot.

Morrison yelled at Barnum, "You stupid brave bastard," And took aim.

Patrick Barnum fought himself free for one moment and seemed to look directly at Morrison. He seemed to have a smile on his face.

Morrison pulled the trigger and put a bullet through his forehead.

When he turned around, slammed the door shut, set the dead bolt and wedged the chair beneath the door knob the Sheriff saw that Buck L. Morrison had a single tear running down his right cheek. But the Sheriff didn't say anything about it.

On this night there was no time for tears.

Killrain was already on his feet and was back shooting faces out of the window when Morrison returned to the cell where Shingi worked on stopping the blood flowing from Clyde's hand and he went back to the dirty business of trying to kill the dead.

Before Shingi even finished bandaging Clyde's bite wound he started shaking uncontrollably.

"I feel like I got fire in my veins," Clyde told Shingi. "What the hell is wrong with me?"

Shingi had never in all her years as a medicine woman for her tribe seen anything like this sickness. It instantly attacked those bitten by these dead people making them suddenly deathly sick and then raving blood-hungry lunatics. She didn't have any answers for Clyde's question. So she was honest with him.

Shingi told Clyde, "I do not know what you just got with that bite but I'll do everything for you that I can."

That was when Morrison, Shingi and Killrain heard the Sheriff yell out over the gunshots, "Everybody! Everything just got a hell of a lot worse. We're going to have to get the hell out of here!"

Killrain glanced over at Morrison then looked back to the window and blasted a big juicy red hole in the center of a face that looked like it had belonged to a hard working farmer before this mess began.

Morrison went in the main room to see what Matt Jackson was talking about.

"Take a look at this," The Sheriff said and pointed with his rifle barrel to a square in the ceiling where small wisps of smoke drifted down. He pushed the square upward with the rifle barrel and a large puff of smoke came into the room. He dropped the square back into place.

"That's my attic," The Sheriff said. "I thought those bastards were mindless but after they couldn't get in through the windows or door they set fire to the roof. Either Abner made them do that or they figured it out on their own."

"It doesn't make a bit of difference how they figured it out," Morrison told him. "Pretty soon, this place will burn down with us in it."

The Sheriff went back to the same closet where he got all the guns from. He pulled an ax out and handed it to Morrison.

"I've already told the Hanson's this. In the middle of the cell you've all been in, beneath the floorboards is a tunnel. Chop those boards out of the way and the four of you can get the hell out of here."

Morrison saw an old Civil War Officer's Sword with a belt and scabbard standing in a corner of the closet. He reached in and took it and buckled the sword around him.

"I might need this pig-sticker," he told the Sheriff.

"You're welcome to it," Matt Jackson said.

"What's going to happen to you?" Morrison asked.

"This is my town," the Sheriff told Morrison. "I feel kind of responsible for all of this. I should have shot that god-dammed Dr. Abner the first time I saw him. I knew there was something bad wrong when he showed up, but I let it be. Look at Totem Lake now.

"I'm riding out everything right here inside my Jail House, all the way to the end."

The way he said that, Morrison knew there wasn't going to be any talking the Sheriff out of what he decided, so he didn't try. Morrison went back into the cell with Shingi and Killrain and told them about the roof burning and started tapping around on the floor boards with the ax head.

In the center of the room his taps made a hollow sound. That was where he started chopping the floor boards up. As he was chopping Carl came in to check on Clyde.

He didn't like what he saw.

"You're going to have to leave me here," Clyde told Carl. "After what happened to that Deputy you know it's gonna happen to me too. It's just a matter of time."

"I ain't leaving you nowhere," Carl told Clyde. "You get that out of your head right now."

The main room was getting thick with smoke by the time Morrison had two boards chopped in half. Killrain took a break from shooting out zombie eyes and helped him pry the floor boards up and toss them off to the side making an opening just big enough for one person to squeeze through.

From the main room came some cursing and a hail of gunshots. They heard something fall hard to the wood floor.

Morrison rushed back in there and saw Sheriff Matt Jackson put another bullet into a zombie that fell from the entrance to the attic.

The Sheriff said, "They must have burned a hole in the roof and are coming in through it. You all best get a move on. I'll hold them here as long as I can."

"It ain't too late for you to come with us," Morrison told him.

The zombiefied face of the owner of Wesley's Gun Smith Shop was thrust down into the open square in the ceiling and looked around for someone to leap on and bite. The Sheriff fired twice into that leering face. Wesley's chin and nose vanished in a red ruin that spurted black blood. He was wedged in the opening to the attic and hung half in and out dripping.

"It is too late!" The Sheriff yelled. "Now get the hell out of here!"

Morrison went back into the cell and handed the lantern to Shingi.

"You go down first," He told her. She started to protest and Morrison said, "We don't have time for this. Just go!"

Shingi slid down through the boards and found a downward sloping walkway that was roughly four feet wide. She could see the roof ahead was about six and a half feet from the floor.

The air smelled musty but a slight breeze blew inward from above indicating that there had to be an exit somewhere ahead for the wind to be blowing through.

"It's alright down here," Shingi shouted up. "Come on down."

Morrison dropped into the hole and had Carl slide Clyde down to him. Then Carl came down with Killrain following him.

Carl insisted on carrying his brother so he slung Clyde's arm over his shoulder and Killrain slung his other arm over his.

When Carl told Killrain, "I can do it on my own." Killrain gave him a look that said *Just shut up and go!* and he did.

Rifle fire came regularly from behind them as Shingi lead the way and the tunnel sloped downward for maybe thirty feet then leveled off to a flat weather beaten walkway. It was obvious to Shingi and Morrison since they were seeing the tunnel sides by the direct light of the lantern that this tunnel had not been dug by any escaping prisoners.

They might have used the tunnel to escape by but this tunnel was here a long time before anyone was in Totem Lake.

Shingi followed the tunnel for maybe fifty yards when behind them the rifle fire suddenly came fast and furious and everyone in the party guessed that Sheriff Matt Jackson was making his last stand.

Then the firing stopped and they heard the sound of collapsing wood. A moment later a warm cloud of smoke passed by, making them momentarily choke and cough.

After that happened Morrison told all of them, "I think the Jail House just caved in."

Then they heard the sound of wood scraping and digging and boards being pried loose.

Killrain said, "They must have seen the opening to this here tunnel before the building collapsed and they're digging it up.

That was when Carl told everyone, "Clyde's dead. He quit breathing a few minutes ago."

Shingi felt for his pulse and said, "He is gone."

"He's my brother. I'm not leaving him," Carl told them.

"You have to," Morrison said. "He'll be waking up in a few minutes and he'll be like the Deputy. You know that."

"Buck with all due respect, I ain't leaving Clyde's side and there ain't anyone that can make me. I'll do what I have to when he wakes up," Carl told them.

"You could never shoot your own brother," Killrain said. "So I'll stay here and do it for you."

He turned to Morrison. "You get your woman out of here," Killrain told him. "I owe you a big one and I reckon this sets everything even."

"Yeah," Morrison said. "I reckon we are even now."

Morrison shook hands with the two of them and Shingi gave Carl a hug and Killrain a handshake.

Killrain told Shingi, "I figured I did deserve that punch to the gut but I sure could have done without that knee to the nuts. That's the place no man likes the get hit."

Shingi answered, "That was why I did it."

Killrain laughed and turned back toward the fight.

It made their hearts heavy in their chests but Shingi and Morrison went on down the tunnel and left the two men to do what they had to do.

* * *

After about fifty more yards of walking in the tunnel it curved upward. From behind them came the sound of a single gunshot, then shouts followed by a whole lot of gun shots fired one right after the other.

Morrison and Shingi knew that the living dead citizens of Totem Lake must have made it down into the tunnel reaching Killrain and Carl just about the same time that Clyde woke up.

The tunnel curved upward and after just a few minutes of climbing Shingi and Morrison was out in the open again breathing clean air.

Directly in front of them less than twenty yards away lay the glistening waters of Totem Lake. The tunnel had come out at the bottom of a cliff face that curved around to the south and lead directly into the lake. Only an extremely acrobatic monkey would be able to climb that cliff and neither Morrison nor Shingi qualified as that.

To the east they could see the sky was lightening with the first bluish coloring of the coming dawn. To the northeast the glow from the burning Jail House could be seen. Between the glow of the Jail House and Morrison and Shingi was the rounded off top of a hill.

A short figure dressed all in black walked to the top of the hill and even from that distance he seemed to look directly at Morrison and Shingi.

It was Dr. Abner.

He pointed and shouted something that Morrison and Shingi could not understand. But it didn't take much imagination to figure out what he was yelling when the hungry dead citizens of Totem Lake came running out of the same tunnel that Morrison and Shingi came out.

Morrison and Shingi both had rifles and they cut down the onrushing zombies as they came. Bullets splattered brains to the wind and the zombies came on until Morrison and Shingi were clicking on empty.

Then Morrison pushed Shingi behind him and pulled the old Civil War Sword that he'd taken from the closet in the Jail House and met the undead charge with naked steel.

Morrison didn't know a dam thing about sword fighting, but he knew how to fight and he didn't know the meaning of quit. So when the zombies came he found a spot next to the cliff face where it was too narrow for more than two of them at a time to come at him.

When they charged he hacked hands and arms off first, then he would remove their heads.

Morrison fought a grim battle protecting Shingi until he felt that his sword arm was on fire from all of the swinging of that old blade and the pain was such that he felt that soon his arm would rip loose out of the socket. How long that grim struggle went on there was no way to know. The sand of the Beach of Totem Lake was stained red as the sky lightened and just as the sun crested the horizon the last two zombies that faced off with Morrison were all too familiar to him.

It was Jake Killrain and Carl Hanson that stood in front of Morrison.

The both of them stood there snarling and growling like rabid dogs with drool dripping from their mouths. A momentary sense of recognition seemed to flash through their faces. Through their distorted dead features, through the fog of the weird binding magic that Abner used to control these animated corpses they seemed to somehow recognize the face of their friend.

Dr. Abner from his hill top shouted again and this time it came clear to Morrison and Shingi's ears, "Kill them!"

Pain etched on the faces of Killrain and Carl as they moved forward to attack.

That was when the sun came bursting up over the horizon.

With the touch of the first rays of the morning sun the animated corpses began to smoke. They hissed and crackled and for Carl and Killrain it looked like an expression of relief washed over their faces when they burst into flames and collapsed onto the beach to burn down to nothing but ash.

Shingi touched Morrison to get his attention as he watched the flaming remains of Carl and Killrain and whispered in his ear, "Dr. Abner is still there."

She pointed to the crest of the hill.

Morrison's answer was simple.

"He needs to die!"

They headed toward the hill and as they approached it something that neither of them understood happened.

Out of the clouds overhead in the light of the morning they saw a dark shaft of pure blackness, something that could only be described as anti-light because it was pure black and seemed to absorb the light around it, shoot down and strike Dr. Abner like a thunderbolt.

There was a black flash, like the opposite of a lightning flash that actually left afterimages of white in front of their eyes before that faded away. Then Morrison and Shingi witnessed a startling transformation.

Dr. Abner screamed, "No!" And seemed to shrink and grow squat and shorter. Then eight hairy legs shot out from his torso. His head disappeared down into his shoulders and he continued to shrink, to grow smaller until he was about the size of a man's hand.

Inside Shingi's head she heard a voice that she knew well. It told her, *"It has been decreed that he can never die but this is how he shall remain for eternity. It is his true nature."*

Dr. Abner had been transformed into a spider.

The Dr. Abner/spider-thing screeched out a cry of terror and rage. It cast a frightened look at its surroundings surveying the trees and grasses wondering what larger predators were out there to make a meal of him and then it scuttled off into the weeds.

When Morrison went to chase him down Shingi put a restraining hand upon his shoulder saying, "He can't hurt anyone now. He has been punished."

Morrison thought that over. He answered, "Yeah, I guess you're right. I wouldn't want to end up as a spider. I guess he'll have to learn to like the taste of bugs."

* * *

They walked back into town and the smoking remnants of the walking dead seemed to be everywhere. The citizens of Totem Lake who had been in hiding were starting to come out into the streets.

Horse was running up and down the street like he was looking for Morrison and came right away when called. They were standing outside the burned down Jail House with Morrison and Shingi petting their loyal animal when they heard a metallic banging from under the pile of collapsed rubble. Then they heard some muffled shouts.

Morrison and Shingi looked at each other. Then Shingi yelled to some of the towns folk, "We need some help over here! Someone's alive in there." She waved at the burned down Jail House.

Ten of the town's men came and dragged pieces of the burned building away and dug through the rubble following the voice to a turned upside down metal gun cabinet. As soon as they got everything cleared out of the way they stood the metal cabinet up and opened the door.

Matt Jackson the Sheriff of Totem Lake fell out of the cabinet and onto the ground. He sucked in a lungful of clean air.

"Jesus Christ!" The Sheriff panted. "It got hotter than hell in there."

He saw Morrison and Shingi.

Morrison told him, "I'm glad you made it through. We figured you were dead."

"Same here," the Sheriff told him. "When I ran low on ammo and everything started coming down on my head I remembered this was in my bedroom. Even then I thought I was gonna cook."

Matt Jackson turned to the group of men watching him. "You all better plan on building a new and better Jail House because I'm staying! How about the two of you, what are you planning on doing?" He asked Morrison and Shingi.

Shingi looked at Morrison and he spoke loud enough so that the small gathering crowd would hear him.

"I don't think that I can settle in any one town just yet. John L Sullivan has a beating coming to him and I'm the man that should be handing that out.

So Shingi and me got a lot of traveling to do and a lot of places ahead of us to see."

The two of then climbed upon Horse.

As they rode out Sheriff Matt Jackson waved and shouted, "Come on back any time. You'll always be welcome here."

"We might," Buck L. Morrison shouted over his shoulder and they rode off into the sunrise because that's how we do it out here in Washington.

In Washington if you ride off into the sunset, unless you can walk on water, you don't get very far.

*   *   *

You might think that this story is over now and in a way it is. You see, Buck L. Morrison never actually did go after the Heavyweight Championship.

John L. Sullivan lost The Heavyweight Championship of The World shortly after what took place in Totem Lake. James J. Corbett, the man who beat Sullivan, from what Morrison read about him, was a guy that was hard to dislike. So he had no great want to kick his ass for him.

Besides, after facing down Night Knuckles and a town full of the hungry living dead those other prize fighters just didn't seem like much of a challenge.

As the story goes Buck L. Morrison and Shingi was married, had a passel of kids and a whole slew of other adventures.

But that is another story to be told on another night.

EPILOGUE
The Rest Haven Nursing Home
Seattle Washington
Present Day

After his tale the old man was exhausted. He'd talked a long time and thanked me for listening.

I told him, "No, thank you! These days no one tells stories anymore. People are always watching too much T.V. to talk very much. People just don't..."

But I saw that the old man had already closed his eyes and his breath came in the regular rhythm of sleep.

I reached out and squeezed his hand.

"Sleep well old dude," I told him.

*　　*　　*

I arrived early to work my next shift at The Rest Haven Nursing Home that night. I wanted to get a head start on my work so I could go by and see if the old man had some more stories to tell.

At the east end of the building an orderly was at work bringing a few cardboard boxes out of the old man's room and stacking them on a cart.

I went to say hello to the old guy and the orderly told me he'd passed away around noon.

"When the nurse came to feed him lunch he was dead," the orderly said.

"Dam," I muttered.

I looked at the boxes on the cart, three large cardboard boxes. Those three very small containers held the contents of a man's entire life.

They were filled with a few personal items, a photo album and lots of old handwritten journals.

"I guess his family will be coming by for those," I said to the orderly.

"He didn't have any family," the orderly told me. "No one ever came to see him. He was just another old and forgotten man."

"Mind if I keep those," I asked pointing at the boxes.

"Knock yourself out," the orderly said. "You know how it is here. I was going to take them to the dumpster."

I wheeled the cart out to my car and put the boxes in the trunk. Later I would take a look at the journals and read what the old man had to say.

If there were stories in there as good as the one the old man had told me the night before, then I'd try to make the old man's voice be heard.

"You said you'd die forgotten and silent," I said to the old man who I felt was somehow looking over my shoulder. "Well, I'll remember you and I'll try to make others remember."

I closed the trunk lid and as I turned to go back to work a tear ran down my face.

AUTHOR'S NOTE

In the original version of this story the names of the two main characters were Bob L. Morgan and Flora Izalia. Those are my parents.

Night Knuckles was written with them as the intended audience so I hope they like it. It was also written as a thank you for having a good childhood.

Thanks Mom & Dad for raising me. After making my own way in this tough as nails world for the last twenty plus years I do appreciate the times when life wasn't a daily struggle.

My childhood was the easy time in my life. I didn't know how easy it was until it was over.

Mom & Dad you are my heroes.

I had to change the names when trying to market this novel for two different reasons. I used to publish under the name of John Dark and have now dropped that pseudonym. Since I am also named Bob L. Morgan it just seemed strange to have a novel with the main character to have the same name as the author. I had done that before with mixed results.

As for the second reason: When it came time to give the two main characters a romantic scene I had a hard time doing it with my parents as the characters doing the action. Maybe that means that I am the product of a virgin birth. Or maybe it just means that there are psychological factors here that I have no understanding of. I don't know. I only know that I enjoyed writing this book and that my parents are the real hero's here. And that's all that does matter.

Wherever your life's journeys may take you, I wish you a happy ending.

Take Care
Have Fun
B. L. Morgan Jr.

VISIT

SPEAKING VOLUMES ONLINE

National Best-Selling

&

Award Winning Authors

www.speakingvolumes.us

www.ingramcontent.com/pod-product-compliance
Lightning Source LLC
Chambersburg PA
CBHW050751250626
47155CB00005B/2011